"I wish all Holmesian pastiche could be as
honest, as knowledgeable, as enthusiastic and
as well written – in short, as good – as these
children's books."

THE SHERLOCK HOLMES SOCIETY OF LONDON

Other Baker Street Boys adventures:

THE CASE OF THE RACEHORSE RINGER

ANTHONY READ

illustrated by

DAVID FRANKLAND

**WALKER
BOOKS**

For Rosemary, as ever, with love

First published 2012 by Walker Books Ltd
87 Vauxhall Walk, London SE11 5HJ

2 4 6 8 10 9 7 5 3 1

Text © 2012 Anthony Read
Illustrations © 2012 David Frankland

The right of Anthony Read and David Frankland to be identified as author
and illustrator respectively of this work has been asserted by them in
accordance with the Copyright, Designs and Patents Act 1988

This book has been typeset in ITC Garamond

Printed and bound in Italy by 🦁 Grafica Veneta S.p.A.

British Library Cataloguing in Publication Data:
a catalogue record for this book is available from the British Library

ISBN 978-1-4063-3524-8

www.walker.co.uk

CONTENTS

"*R*ight," *the man rasped. "Out you come. We're here.*"

He threw open the door of the horsebox, reached inside and grabbed Gertie's arm with a grip like an iron band. Gertie blinked as he dragged her out into the street. It had been dark in the back of the van, and now she was out in the daylight everything seemed too bright.

"Where's here?" she asked.

"Your new home," the man said.

As her eyes adjusted to the light, Gertie saw that they were standing outside a grim, grey building behind tall iron railings.

"It don't look much like home to me." She sniffed. "Looks more like a blinkin' prison."

"What do you want? Roses round the door?"

"Sure and that'd be nice." Gertie grinned.

"Pink and white would do just fine."

"Cheeky little devil!"

"I ain't goin' in there."

"Oh yes you are. Come on!"

He tightened his grip on her arm and began to drag her through the gate. Gertie yelped in pain, but there was no way she could escape.

The man yanked on an iron handle at the side of the front door, and a bell clanged somewhere inside the building. After what seemed like an age, Gertie heard footsteps approaching. There was the sound of a key grating in the lock and the heavy door creaked open. A hard-faced woman stood facing them.

"What's this?" she demanded through thin lips. "Major Lee told me it was a girl."

"It is a girl. This is Gertie O'Grady."

The woman glared at Gertie. Gertie glared back. Neither of them liked what they saw. Gertie saw a big woman in a long black dress, buttoned high up at the neck, with a large bunch of keys dangling from her belt. The woman's pale eyes moved down from Gertie's cropped ginger hair and freckled face, taking in *her ragged jacket, tattered boy's trousers and bare toes poking out of well-worn boots. She did not try to hide her dislike.*

"Where are her things?" she asked the man.

"I ain't got none," Gertie said. "My stuff was in our wagon and the coppers—"

"Be quiet!" the woman barked. "Who said you could speak?"

"You asked about my things—"

"And don't answer back! In this house you speak when you're spoken to, and not before. Understand?"

"Sure and I was only—"

"Hold your tongue, miss!"

The woman slapped her, hard, on the side of the head. Gertie glowered at her in silence.

"I can see we've a lot to teach you before you'll fit in here," the woman sighed. She nodded curtly to the man. "Very well, Hogg. You may go."

"Thank you, madam." He let go of Gertie's arm and stepped away. "She's all yours – and the best of luck to both of you."

When he had gone, the woman closed the

door behind him and locked it. Then she walked slowly around Gertie, inspecting her carefully.

"My name is Mrs Hackett," she announced. "I am the matron of this orphanage."

"I ain't a orphan, missus," Gertie began. "I got—"

"Quiet! What did I tell you? Speak when you are spoken to, and address me at all times as Matron or Mrs Hackett. Do you understand?"

"Yes, missus. Er, Matron."

"That's better." Mrs Hackett turned and yelled down the hallway as loud as a steam whistle. "Ethel! Sarah!"

Her voice was still echoing round the walls when two young women wearing long aprons and mob-caps scuttled out of a doorway. Mrs Hackett shoved Gertie towards them.

"Clean her up!" she snarled. "And get rid of those filthy rags!"

The next half-hour was one of the worst Gertie had ever known. Ethel and Sarah grabbed an arm each and hauled her up the stairs and into a bare, grey room, in the middle of which stood a large bathtub filled with water. Gertie had never seen a bath before, and she feared this was some sort of torture chamber. Her fears were soon justified.

The two maids roughly pulled off her clothes, then dragged her towards the bath. Gertie kicked and bit and scratched and yelled, but it was no use: they picked her up and plunged her in. Gertie was used to cold water – ever since she was little she had swum in rivers and lakes and ponds. But this was so cold that it took her breath away. When she got it back again, she screamed louder than ever. Ethel and Sarah shut her up by pushing her head under the water, then attacking her with bars of hard, foul-smelling yellow soap and scrubbing her all over until her skin was red and raw.

At last they pulled her, shivering, out of the water, rubbed her dry with a rough towel and thrust a small pile of clothes at her.

"Now put these on," Ethel ordered. "And look sharp about it. Mrs Hackett don't like to be kept waiting."

Gertie stared at the clothes. A coarse woollen

vest, navy-blue knickers, black knitted stock-
ings, canvas shoes, a white mob-cap ... and a
thick grey cotton dress.

"I don't wear frocks," she said.

"You do here," Sarah replied. "That's the
uniform."

"What's a uniform?"

"It's what everybody has to wear. So put it on
and shut up."

"No! I won't!" Gertie folded her arms and
shook her head.

"What's going on here?" a harsh voice barked
out. "And what's taking so long?"

Mrs Hackett stood in the doorway, her face
like stone. As she stepped forwards, Gertie saw
that she was holding a length of bamboo with a
hooked handle. A cane. It made a humming noise
as the matron swished it through the air.

"Get dressed!" she hissed. "Now!"

Bravely, Gertie shook her head again. The
matron raised the cane and whacked her on
the back of her leg. The pain came as a shock to
Gertie. But she clenched her teeth and did not
cry out, staring defiantly at her attacker.

"Hold her!" Mrs Hackett told the two maids. "Hold her tight while I give her the beating she deserves."

"Just you wait!" Gertie cried angrily. "Just you wait till my da comes for me. He'll show you what for!"

"Your da won't be coming for you," Mrs Hackett sneered. "He's never coming. Your precious da is a murderer. And he's going to hang!"

ESCAPE

Rosie was carrying the day's flowers from Covent Garden market back to HQ, the secret cellar where she and the other Baker Street Boys lived. It was still early and the streets of London were empty. Behind her, the clip-clop of a horse's hooves cut through the quietness, slowing from a trot to a walk and then stopping altogether. Rosie turned and saw it was Mr Gorman, the local dairyman, bringing large silver churns of milk from the farm in his pony and trap. He had a passenger with him, a strange-looking girl in a grey dress.

"Rosie!" the strange girl shrieked. She leapt from the trap and hurled herself at the flower girl, throwing her arms around her.

"Oi! Mind my flowers. Who d'you think you are?"

"Don't you know me, then?"

Rosie certainly knew the voice. Her mouth dropped open.

"Oh my word! Gertie! What happened to you?"

"I'll tell you all about it when we get to HQ." Gertie turned back to the milkman in his peaked cap and long striped apron. "Ta, Mr Gorman. Thanks for the ride."

Mr Gorman waved and started his horse again. The two girls hurried back to HQ.

Queenie was dishing out porridge to the rest of the Boys – Wiggins, Beaver, Shiner and Sparrow – when Rosie and Gertie clattered down the steps and into the cellar. Porridge for breakfast was a rare treat, and no one looked up from their battered tin plates to see who had come in until Rosie called out.

"Look who I found," she said.

Five pairs of eyes turned to the doorway and stared at the newcomer. For a moment no one said anything. Then Shiner saw who it was and started to laugh. The others joined in, apart from Queenie, who could see that Gertie was upset and close to tears. She put down her serving spoon, hurried over and put an arm round her shoulders.

"Gertie, love," she said gently. "What's happened? What's up?"

Gertie bit her lip, then took a deep breath.

"It's my da," she said. "He's in prison."

"Again?" Wiggins grinned. "What's he done this time? More poaching? Tickling a few trout?"

"No. He ain't done nothin'. But they say he's a murderer. And they're goin' to hang him."

The laughter stopped. Everyone was shocked into silence.

"Come and sit down," Queenie said. "Have some breakfast and you can tell us all about it."

The Boys shuffled round and made room for Gertie at the table.

"Now then," said Wiggins. "First things first. Who's your da s'posed to have murdered?"

"A lad at Major Lee's racin' stables."

"What's a racin' stables?" Shiner asked.

"It's where they train racehorses, stupid," said Sparrow.

"Who you callin' stupid?"

"That's enough," Queenie cut in quickly. "We don't need you two squabblin'. This is serious."

"Right," agreed Wiggins. "Now, Gertie, I need to know everything."

"He didn't do it. Not my da. He don't mind killin' a rabbit or a pheasant – for the pot, like. We have to eat. But not a lad, like Tommie. He would never do that. He couldn't."

"Is Tommie the lad what was killed?"

"Yes."

"Did you know him, then?"

"A bit. I'd see him exercisin' the horses. It's what the lads do – they look after the horses, feed 'em, groom 'em, ride 'em out. And sometimes, when he'd finished work for the day, he'd come to the woods where we had our wagon parked."

"What'd he come for?" Wiggins asked.

"Sure and it was just to get away from the stables for an hour."

"He wasn't happy there, then?"

"He loved the horses, but the other lads, and the trainer – if you ask me, they used to knock him about a bit."

"You mean they bullied him?"

"They did so. Black and blue he was sometimes."

Wiggins got up from the table and began pac-
ing the room, deep in thought. As the others
finished their porridge, they watched and
waited. Wiggins was their leader. If someone had
a problem, he could usually think of a solution.
He had learned a lot from working for the great
detective, Mr Sherlock Holmes.

At last he stopped and turned back to Gertie.

"What was you and your da doing there?" he
asked.

"Watchin' the lads ridin' the racehorses on the
gallops."

"What's the gallops?"

"It's where the horses can run flat out. You
know, first they walk, then they trot, then they
canter and then they gallop, fast as they can go."

"Why d'you want to watch 'em?"

"So we could time 'em."

"How?"

"With a stopwatch, of course. There's this
fella, see. He give my da a stopwatch, and he was

payin' him to time the horses, to see which was the fastest."

"Why would he want to know that?" asked Beaver, looking puzzled.

"So he'd know which one to bet his money on," said Wiggins.

"That's right," Gertie answered. "The one that was goin' to win when they went into a race."

Beaver let out a low whistle of admiration. "Cor," he said, "you could get rich if you knew that."

The other Boys nodded in agreement.

"Yes. Very clever," said Wiggins. "Who is this geezer, Gert?"

Gertie shook her head. "I dunno. I never seen him. My da said he was called Slippery Sam or some such. They always met up in secret."

"Secret, eh?" Wiggins thought for a moment. "The lad what was killed…"

"Tommie."

"Yeah, Tommie. Could he have found out the secret? Could that be why he was murdered?"

Gertie shrugged. "Dunno. All I know is, it weren't my da what did it."

Wiggins paced the floor again for a moment.

"Could your dad have an alibi?" he asked.

"What's an alibi?"

"It's when somebody couldn't have done a crime 'cos they can prove they was somewhere else."

"He was with me."

"That's no good. You're his daughter – they won't believe you."

"But it's true."

"*We* know that, but the coppers won't. They'll think you'd say anything to get him off."

"I would if it was my dad," Sparrow piped up. "If I had a dad, that is."

The other Boys all agreed, and sat in silence for a while, thinking about the families they might have had. Then Queenie cleared her throat and turned to Wiggins.

"Well," she said, "if we can't prove he *didn't* do it, there's only one thing we can do. Prove who *did*."

"Exac'ly," said Wiggins. "That's exac'ly what we've gotta do. We gotta find the real murderer."

"How we gonna do that, then?" asked Shiner.

"Dunno yet. First thing, we'll go and see Mr Holmes."

Five minutes later, the seven Baker Street Boys were standing outside 221b Baker Street. Wiggins rang the bell, and the door was opened by Billy, Mrs Hudson's pageboy. Billy had been eating his breakfast and was busy trying to fasten the many buttons on his jacket – and getting them in a tangle.

"Oh, it's you lot!" He scowled. "What do you want at this time of day?"

"We gotta see Mr Holmes," Wiggins told him. "It's urgent. Matter of life and death."

"Well, you'll have to die, then," Billy replied. "He ain't here."

"Do you know where he is? When he'll be back?"

Billy shook his head and started to close the door. Wiggins quickly stuck his foot in the gap to stop him.

"In that case, we'll see Dr Watson. Is he in?"

Billy sighed. "Wait here."

While they were waiting on the doorstep, the

Boys heard a familiar cry: "Milko! Milko!" and Mr Gorman stopped his pony and trap beside the kerb. A kitchen maid came out of the next house, carrying a large white jug. Mr Gorman lifted the lid off the churn in his trap, and ladled milk into the jug. Most of the houses around Baker Street now bought their milk in the new-fangled bottles from the big dairy company, but some still liked to have it delivered in the old-fashioned way by Mr Gorman.

When he had finished serving the maid, the milkman gave Gertie a friendly smile.

"You found your friends OK, then?" he called to her.

"Yes, thank you," she answered. "And thanks again for the ride."

"Any time," he said. He clicked his tongue at his horse to tell it to walk on, though it knew exactly when to move on and when to stop without being told. His call rang down the street as they carried on their way. "Milko! Milko–o–o!"

Billy reappeared in the doorway. "The doctor says you can come up if it's urgent," he said. "But just two of you."

* * *

Dr Watson was finishing a breakfast of kippers and toast when Billy showed Wiggins and Gertie into the room. He carefully moved a kipper's skeleton to the side of his plate and popped the last bit of fish into his mouth. One of the tiny bones had become caught in his moustache and it waggled when he spoke. Wiggins gave a small cough and touched his own upper lip. The doctor reddened and cleared his throat. "Ah, right you are," he said, hurriedly wiping his mouth with his napkin before taking a sip of coffee.

"Now then," he said. "What's so urgent?"

"It's Gertie's dad…" Wiggins began.

"Ah, yes. I remember him from the fairground on Hampstead Heath." The doctor smiled at the memory of a successful investigation. "Splendid chap. He recovered the stolen plans, right?"

"Right."

"What's the problem?"

"They're going to hang him."

"Oh my goodness. Why?"

"They say he's done a murder," Gertie blurted out. "But he ain't."

"And we need Mr Holmes to prove it," Wiggins added.

"I see." The smile disappeared from the doctor's face and was replaced by a serious expression. "I'm afraid Mr Holmes is working on a case in Germany, and I don't know when he'll be back."

"Oh, Lor'! What we gonna do, then?"

"Have you spoken to the police?"

"No, we only just found out – when Gertie come home."

"Came home from where?"

"From the orphanage," Gertie told him.

"The *orphanage*? Is that why you're wearing those clothes, young Gertie?"

"They made me wear 'em," she explained. "They took my own things away and burnt 'em."

"I see." He nodded sympathetically. "What were you doing in an orphanage?"

Gertie pulled a face at the memory, took a deep breath and then told him the whole story. The police, she said, had arrested her father in the middle of the night. The racehorse trainer, Major Lee, had led them to the caravan. When the police took her father away, the major told them he would look after her. But in fact he and his assistant, Harry Hogg, had taken her back to the racing stables and locked her in an empty stall for the rest of the night. Next day, they had chucked her onto the dirty straw in the back of a horsebox, and Hogg had driven her to the orphanage, where he handed her over to the awful Mrs Hackett.

Even when she was cleaned up and dressed, Gertie had not been allowed to see any of the other girls in the orphanage. Instead, they had shut her up in a small room in the attic, with just a narrow iron bed and one rickety wooden chair. Still smarting from her beating by Mrs Hackett, she had made up her mind to escape as soon as she could. But when she tried the door, she had found it was firmly locked. The only window was a skylight in the sloping ceiling. It did not look as though it was locked, but it was too high for her, even when she stood on the chair. Refusing to be beaten, she dragged the bed across the room, put the chair on it and tried again. It was a bit wobbly, but now she could reach the sky-light, open it and put her head out.

At first, all she could see was roof. Then she heard voices from somewhere below. Craning her neck, she looked down and saw two people walking across the yard of the orphanage towards the back gate, where a saddled horse stood waiting patiently. One was Mrs Hackett, the other was a wiry man wearing a flat cap, a ginger tweed jacket and riding breeches. He walked with a stick, limping on one leg, which was shorter than the other. Gertie recognized him as Major Lee, the trainer. They were talking busily, but Gertie could not hear what they were saying until Lee mounted his horse, ready to leave.

"Keep her out of the way until it's all over," Gertie had heard him say. "Then we'll decide what to do with her."

Wiggins and Dr Watson had been listening in horror to Gertie's tale.

"Blimey," said Wiggins, "I don't like the sound of that."

"No, nor do I," agreed the doctor. "I can quite see why you wanted to get away. But how on earth did you manage it?"

"I waited till night-time so nobody'd see me,"

Gertie replied, "then I climbed out of the sky-light and crawled across the roof till I came to a drainpipe. After that it was easy."

"Easy, you say?"

"Yeah," Gertie replied. "All I had to do then was shin down the drainpipe, cross the yard and climb over the fence."

"Amazing!" Dr Watson shook his head in astonishment.

"Our Gertie can climb anything," Wiggins said proudly. "Good as any monkey, she is."

"Yes, I remember." The doctor smiled. "So, Gertie, you got away. Then what did you do?"

"I started walkin', fast as I could. Back to Baker Street and the Boys. It was a long way, but I was lucky – I met Mr Gorman."

"Who?" The doctor looked puzzled.

"Mr Gorman the milkman. You know, he's got the dairy shop just round the corner."

"Oh yes. What was he doing there?"

"Turns out he goes to a farm past there every mornin' in his horse and trap, to collect his milk for the day. So when I seen him I shouted out to him, and he give me a ride all the way home."

"That was a bit of luck."

"It was so," Gertie said fervently. "It's a long walk."

"And did you tell Mr Gorman what had happened?" asked the doctor.

"Only that they'd tried to shut me up in a orphanage, even though I'm not a orphan. I wanted to talk to Wiggins first. And Mr Holmes, of course."

"Quite right."

"But Mr Holmes ain't here," said Wiggins. "So what we gonna do?"

Dr Watson stood up, brushing toast crumbs from his waistcoat. "You must speak to the police," he said firmly.

"But they won't listen to me," Gertie groaned. "I know they won't."

"I shall make sure that Inspector Lestrade does listen," the doctor assured her. He reached for his overcoat, bowler hat and umbrella. "Come along – we shall go to see him at once."

At Scotland Yard, Inspector Lestrade did indeed listen carefully to what Gertie had to say, after sending a sergeant to fetch the file on the case. He stroked his lean, blue-tinged chin with his square-tipped fingers as he thought.

"This orphanage," he said. "Where exactly is it?"

"You ain't gonna try and send me back there, are you?" Gertie asked.

"I don't think we need to," the inspector replied. "Not now you're safely back with your friends."

"Oh, she is," said Wiggins. "She's got Queenie and me, and the rest of the Boys. We all look after one another."

"I can vouch for that." Dr Watson nodded.

"What about school?" the inspector asked sternly.

"I don't have to go to school," Gertie said quickly. "I'm thirteen."

Lestrade looked at her suspiciously, with a very official face, then nodded. "Very well. Now, the orphanage?"

"I can't *tell* you where it is. I could probably take you there, though."

"That won't be necessary," the inspector replied. "As far as I can tell, they've done nothing wrong. They took you into their care, cleaned you up, fed you, clothed you…"

Gertie snorted indignantly and looked down at the dress. "I didn't want their frock. I want my own clothes, but they burnt 'em."

"Probably the best thing to do with them," the inspector said acidly, comparing her clean grey dress with Wiggins's ragged outfit.

"Never mind the clothes," Wiggins interrupted. "What about Gertie's dad?"

"What about him?"

"Are you gonna let him go?"

Lestrade looked surprised. He glanced quickly at the papers in the file on his desk.

"Why should we do that?" he asked.

"'Cos he didn't do it," Gertie said. "He's got an alibaba-whatsit."

"Alibi," Wiggins supplied.

"Really?" The inspector leant forwards with interest. "And what would that be?"

"He was with me," Gertie told him.

"Where?"

"In our wagon, of course. Our caravan."

"All night?"

"Is that when it happened?" Wiggins asked. "In the night?"

"Yes," the inspector replied, then turned back to Gertie. "So you and your father were in your caravan all night. Was anybody else with you?"

"No. Course not."

"I see. Well, it's a brave try. But I'm afraid it won't do."

"Why not?" Wiggins asked.

"Because someone else saw him in the woods, where the lad was murdered."

"Who?" Gertie demanded. "Who says they saw him?"

"I can't tell you that," said the inspector. "It's evidence."

"Well, whoever it is, they're lying."

"And you're not?" he snapped, subjecting her to a fierce glare.

"No!"

Lestrade shrugged his shoulders and shook his head.

"I'm sorry, young lady, but you're going to have to prove it. Until then, you're just wasting my time – and my time is precious." He stood up, indicating that the interview was over.

"How we gonna prove it?" Gertie pleaded.

"That's up to you. But it's the only way you can save your father."

A Hideout in the Woods

Back at HQ, the Boys were glum. While the others had been waiting anxiously for Wiggins and Gertie to come back from Scotland Yard, they had thought that Inspector Lestrade might offer Gertie some help in saving her father. But he had dashed her hopes when he said that someone had seen Patrick O'Grady in the woods where the lad was murdered.

"He didn't say they'd seen him do it, though, did he?" Gertie said.

"No, he didn't," agreed Wiggins.

"And anyways," Gertie went on, "he wasn't there. Whoever it was, they're tellin' lies."

"So why would they do that?" Wiggins asked.

"'Cos they've got summat to hide!" Beaver cried.

"Exac'ly! And what could that be?"

"The identity of the guilty party!" Sparrow exclaimed.

"Who's havin' a party?" asked Rosie, puzzled.

"Nobody," said Queenie. "That's just a way of sayin' the geezer what done it."

"Well, why didn't you say that to start with?" asked Shiner.

"Never mind that," Wiggins said impatiently. "I gotta think about this. Really think."

"Right," said Queenie. "Rosie, I'll give you a hand with your flowers. The rest of you, hop it."

"Not afore I've got out of this frock," Gertie said. "I ain't goin' out in the street lookin' like this."

"All right. See what you can find in the clothes box."

Gertie rummaged through the clothes that the Boys used as spares or disguises. When she had found a jacket and a pair of trousers that were not too tattered, she exchanged them for the hated dress.

"That's more like it," Beaver chuckled as the transformation was completed.

"Now we've got our Gertie back." Sparrow grinned.

When the others had left, Queenie and Rosie settled down quietly to making up the little bunches of flowers – nosegays and posies and buttonholes – for Rosie to sell from her tray.

Wiggins moved over to his special armchair, which he had made from bits and pieces collected from other people's cast-off furniture. It looked odd, but it was very comfortable – in fact, it was often quite hard not to go to sleep in it. Once he was settled, Wiggins could let his mind get to work for hours without interruption. Sometimes he would even put on one of Mr Holmes's old deerstalker hats and suck on a curly pipe, just like the famous detective. Except, of course, Wiggins never put any tobacco in his.

When Queenie and Rosie had finished making up the little bunches of flowers, Rosie arranged them on her tray, then set off for the street to start selling them. But still Wiggins sat in his chair, deep in thought. From time to time he would lift the deerstalker and scratch his head, or rub his hand over his chin, stroking an imaginary beard. Then at last he suddenly sat up and banged his hands down on the arms of the chair.

"Eureka!" he shouted.

"What?" Queenie asked, startled.

"Eureka! It's what Mr Holmes said in the haunted horrors case. When Gertie's dad dug up the box with the plans in it and I opened it."

"Oh yeah," Queenie said. "I sort of remember."

"It's ancient Greek and it means 'I've found it!'"

"Right. And have you?"

"Maybe. Get the others back. They won't have gone far. Get 'em back and I'll tell you."

Wiggins waved his pipe at the other Boys.

"Listen careful, now," he told them. "The coppers ain't gonna help us, so it's up to us to save Gertie's dad. Right?"

The others nodded but still looked puzzled.

"We can't do nothing from here," Wiggins went on. "We gotta get to the scene of the crime."

"You mean Major Lee's racin' stables?" asked Gertie.

"Exac'ly."

"How we gonna do that? It's a long way away," said Beaver.

"We get a ride, like Gertie did."

"From Mr Gorman?" Queenie asked.

"You got it. He goes up near there every morning."

"But his trap ain't that big. And if he's got the milk churns aboard, he'll never get all of us in."

"No, but there'd be room for three of us. Me, Gertie … and Sparrow."

The other Boys looked disappointed. This was going to be an adventure and they did not want to miss it.

"Why you three?" Shiner demanded. "What's wrong with the rest of us?"

"Well," Wiggins answered, "I gotta go because I'm in charge of the investigation. Right?"

Shiner nodded.

"And Gertie's gotta go because she's the only one what knows where everything is. And anyways, we're doing this for her dad."

"But what about Sparrow?"

"Sparrow's gotta go because he's the littlest."

"What's that gotta do with it?" said Shiner.

"If you'll just shut up for a minute, I'll tell you."

"Yes, shut up, Shiner," Sparrow said impatiently. "I wanna know."

Wiggins explained how most stable lads want to become jockeys. They want to ride horses and win races. And to be a jockey, you need to be small – the smaller the better. Big people, he said, weigh more than small ones and the less weight a horse has to carry on its back, the faster it can run.

"Imagine," Wiggins told Shiner, "if I asked you to run up the road, fast as you can. Then I put a bag of bricks on your back and asked you to do it again. It wouldn't half slow you down."

"Sparrow ain't gonna ride in a race, is he?" Beaver asked.

"No," Wiggins replied. "But he's gonna be a stable lad. So he's gotta look like he *could* be a jockey."

"Hang on a minute," Sparrow butted in. "What d'you mean, I'm gonna be a stable lad?"

"Well, if we're gonna find anything out, we need somebody inside the stables," Wiggins explained. "The best person would be Gertie, of course. She knows about horses and riding. But Major Lee knows who she is. And she's a girl, so they wouldn't give her a job anyway."

"That's true," said Beaver. "'Cept how do you know there's a job goin'?"

Wiggins sighed heavily. "Because they just lost a lad, didn't they?"

"You mean Tommie?"

"Exac'ly. The lad what was murdered. They're gonna need a replacement for him, aren't they? So if Sparrow turns up telling 'em he's looking for a job…"

"But I don't know nothin' about horses and stables," protested Sparrow.

"Don't worry," said Gertie, "they'll learn you."

"Teach you," Queenie corrected her.

"What will I have to do?" Sparrow asked.

"Just do as you're told," said Gertie. "Bit of muckin' out, feedin', waterin', groomin'. Whatever they tell you."

"No, I meant what will I have to do about Gertie's dad?"

"Just keep your eyes and ears open," Wiggins

said. "You're gonna be *my* eyes and ears inside those stables."

"But where will *you* be?"

"Me and Gertie—"

"Gertie and I," Queenie corrected him automatically.

"Gertie and me will be staying in her caravan in the woods."

That evening, as it was getting dark, Wiggins, Gertie and Sparrow walked round to Mr Gorman's dairy. They had been to see him earlier in the day, and he had agreed to give them a ride out to the farm when he went to collect his milk. Because he set out so early, he said they could sleep in his stable behind the shop, to be ready to leave with him in the morning. Luckily there were two stalls in the stable. Mr Gorman's horse, Betsy, lived in one of them. The three Boys bedded down in the other, making themselves quite comfortable on bales of straw and hay.

It was still dark when Mr Gorman came to wake them up. Mrs Gorman kindly brought them mugs of milk and hunks of bread and cheese for breakfast. Not knowing when they would eat again, Wiggins stuffed some of it in his pocket, and they wolfed the rest down hungrily while the milkman led Betsy out and harnessed her up. He loaded the empty churns into the trap and the Boys climbed aboard. Then they were off, trotting briskly through the empty London streets.

As dawn began to light up the sky, the pony and trap passed the edge of Hampstead Heath. Soon they were passing through the city's northern suburbs, where the houses were less crowded. Then they reached fields, with cows grazing peacefully in them, and knew they were really in the country now. Mr Gorman stopped at the entrance to a farm.

"This is as far as I go," he told the children. "But the racing stables are only two or three miles further on."

The three Boys climbed out of the trap and thanked him.

"You're very welcome," Mr Gorman said. "I only wish I could do more to help. But I've got to get my milk back to Baker Street before breakfast. If you need me, though, I'm here at this time every morning."

Gertie stroked Betsy's neck and gave her a final pat. Then they waved goodbye and set off along the road. Before long the Boys passed through a village, and then they were in open heathland. Gertie pointed to a cluster of buildings set in a small valley below them.

"There it is," she said. "That's the stables."

Wiggins and Sparrow followed her finger and saw a handsome brick and flint house facing a square yard. It was lined with low wooden buildings with black-painted doors that each divided in two.

"Are those the horses' stables?" Wiggins asked.

"They call 'em loose boxes," Gertie told him.

"Loose?" said Wiggins. "How come?"

"Dunno. I s'pose it's 'cos the horses ain't tied up inside 'em. They can move about, turn round, lie down, do what they like."

Three lads had just entered the yard and were opening the top halves of the doors. Horses' heads appeared in the openings, looking around with interest. They greeted the morning with snorts and whinnies, puffing steaming breath from their nostrils.

"Aren't they just beautiful?" Gertie said.

Sparrow wasn't so sure. He was used to horses in the street, pulling cabs or carriages or delivery vans. Like the rest of the Boys, he sometimes earned a few pennies holding horses' heads outside shops, to stop them wandering off while their owners went inside to make purchases. Those horses were usually pretty docile. But these were different. They tossed their heads impatiently, eager to be out of their stalls.

He swallowed nervously. "They look very lively," he said.

"Sure and haven't they just had a good night's sleep," Gertie answered. "They can't wait to get onto the gallops."

"Will I have to ride 'em?"

"Not to start with, I don't s'pose."

"Come on," Wiggins interrupted. "We should get away from here before anybody spots Gertie."

"Good thinkin'," said Gertie. "I don't want to end up in that orphanage again."

"Where's your caravan?" Wiggins asked.

"It's tucked away in the woods, like a hideout. I'll show you."

After climbing over the top of a steep hill, the three Boys entered the leafy woods. The bright morning disappeared immediately. The trees were packed close together, shutting out the daylight and casting a heavy shade. Some of them were twisted into strange shapes, like primeval monsters or evil witches, and it was easy to imagine ogres lurking in the shadows or strange creatures skulking in the ancient hollow trunks. Sparrow shivered. Even Wiggins glanced nervously around him. But Gertie did not seem to be worried at all.

She led them through the woods until they came to a clearing, in the middle of which stood the caravan, looking abandoned.

"Where's your horse?" Wiggins asked.

"Major Lee must've took her," Gertie said. "I expect they'll be usin' her at the stables."

"That's stealin'!" Sparrow exclaimed.

"Better than leaving her here on her own with nobody to look after her," Wiggins pointed out.

"It's still stealin'," Sparrow insisted. "I'll look out for her when I'm there."

"Good lad," said Gertie. "Her name's Patch. You'll know her 'cos she's a skewbald."

"What, she's got no hair?"

"No, not bald. Skewbald. Three colours – white, brown and black. You'll not see many of them in a racin' stables. All the others will be thoroughbreds."

Gertie climbed the steps to the caravan door. It was not locked. She opened it and stepped inside. The other two followed.

"It's very cosy," said Wiggins.

"And tidy," added Sparrow.

"You have to be tidy when this is all the space you have," Gertie told him. "A place for everythin' and everythin' in its place. That's what my ma used to say." And indeed everything was in its place. There were two narrow beds, one on either side, which served as seats during the day. Between them was a small folding table and under them were cupboards and drawers. Everything was painted in bright colours and decorated with lots of flowers.

"It's just like that canal boat we went on to Limehouse," Sparrow said. "'Cept this one ain't goin' nowhere."

Wiggins looked around carefully, in case there were any clues to be found. But he could not see anything that looked unusual.

"Is anything missing?" he asked.

Gertie shook her head. "Don't think so. Wait a minute, though. If they was goin' to take any-thin'…" She opened a cupboard and looked inside. "No. Still there."

Inside the cupboard were a stopwatch, a pair of powerful binoculars and a notebook and pencil.

"Spyglasses!" Wiggins exclaimed. "And good ones by the look of 'em. Where did your dad get these?"

"This fella give 'em to him."

"The one who wanted him to time the horses?"

"That's right. Along with this stopwatch."

Wiggins picked up the binoculars. "Let's see if they're any good." He stepped outside the caravan and held them up to his eyes. "Can't tell. Too many trees."

"Come over here, then," Gertie said, leading him to the edge of the woods. Here, the ground sloped steeply away, opening up a good view of the heathland below. Gertie pointed. "That's the gallops, down there."

Wiggins raised the glasses again and looked through them.

"Phew!" He let out a whistle. "You can't half see everything. These must've cost a packet. Whatever this geezer's up to, it's gotta be worth a lot of money."

"Let's have a look," Sparrow begged. Wiggins handed over the binoculars and showed him how to focus the lenses. Sparrow scanned the heathland below them. "Cor!" he exclaimed with delight. "I can see every single blade of grass down there... Hello, what's this?"

A line of horses approached along the track from the stables, each ridden by a lad wearing riding breeches and a flat cap. Leading them, on a big chestnut horse, was a thin man in a tweed jacket.

"That's him," said Gertie. "That's Major Lee, the trainer."

"Why is he a major? He ain't in the army, is he?"

"My da said he used to be. But he broke his leg and had to retire. That's when he bought the stables."

"I see," Wiggins said. "Keep back in the trees, out of sight."

The three Boys watched as the riders, under the stern eye of the trainer, began to put the horses through their paces. One after another they trotted, cantered, then galloped. The last horse was easily the fastest – and the most beautiful, with a glossy black coat, a white blaze in the middle of his forehead and what looked like white socks on his front legs.

"Ain't he beautiful?" Gertie said. "Look at him go! That's Silver Star. He's the best racehorse in the country."

"I dare say," said Wiggins. "Oh, look – they got company."

While the Boys had been looking at the horses they had not noticed a carriage approaching along the track. It stopped so that whoever was in it could watch the horses exercising. Wiggins stared at it and stiffened. He reached out and took the binoculars from Sparrow, then trained them on the carriage door.

"Well I never…" he murmured. "Now, what's *he* up to here?"

"Who?" asked Sparrow.

"Take a look."

Sparrow did. At first everything was blurred, but as he adjusted the powerful lenses a monogram came into sharp focus on the door of the carriage. It was a curly letter "M".

"Moriarty!" He gasped.

The three Boys stared at each other, aghast. Moriarty was the master criminal who had been the brains behind several of their previous cases. He was the sworn enemy of Sherlock Holmes, who described him as "the Napoleon of crime".

"If Moriarty's mixed up in this," Wiggins said, "it's gotta be something big."

"Yeah, like murder," Gertie added. "And gettin' my da hanged for somethin' he didn't do."

A New Stable Lad

Sparrow walked nervously towards the entrance to the stable yard. He could not help thinking that if a boy had been murdered here, and Gertie's dad had not done it, then whoever had must still be around. Taking a deep breath, he lifted the latch and opened the gate.

Before he could take another step, he was stopped in his tracks by an ear-shattering blast of ferocious barking. A dark shape was hurtling across the yard straight towards him. Sparrow froze, his heart pounding. He was done for! He shrank back against the gate, pressing himself into the slats, away from the savage dog. Then, just before it reached him, it was jerked to a sudden halt. It was chained! If its chain had been even a few inches longer, it would have been able to sink its teeth into him. Still snarling and snapping, the dog was on its hind legs, its red eyes level with his own, strings of saliva dripping from its jaws.

Suddenly a shrill voice ordered, "Satan! Leave! Quiet now."

The dog stopped barking and sank down onto the ground, where it continued to growl, its eyes fixed on Sparrow. Still shaking, Sparrow turned *his* eyes towards the house, where the voice had come from. A girl who was perhaps a couple of years older than himself was standing in the doorway, wiping her hands on her flowery pinafore and smiling at him through sparkling grey eyes.

"He had you going there, didn't he," she said.

Sparrow nodded.

"Nearly wet yourself, I'll bet."

Sparrow shook his head. "No," he lied.

"I wouldn't blame you if you did."

"Does he have to be so fierce?" asked Sparrow, his heartbeat slowly returning to normal.

"That's what he's here for. He's a guard dog, see?"

"What's he guardin'?"

"The stables, of course. Some of our horses are worth hundreds and hundreds."

"Hundreds?" Sparrow's eyes nearly popped out of his head. "You mean hundreds of *pounds*?"

"That's right. Now then, who are you and what d'you want?" asked the girl.

Sparrow thought hard, trying to remember everything that Wiggins and Gertie had told him to say.

"My name's Sparrow," he said, "and I want to be a jockey."

"Sparrow? What sort of name's that?"

"It's 'cos I'm not very big," he explained.

"No, you're not, are you?" She laughed, but it wasn't mocking or unfriendly. "Come over here."

Sparrow edged towards her, keeping his back against the gate and his eyes fixed firmly on the dog. It watched his every move intently. When he reached the girl, she looked him up and down, sizing him up.

"Well, you're little enough, that's for sure. Know anything about horses?"

"Not much. But I'm keen to learn."

"Well, we'll have to see what my pa's got to say. He owns these stables."

She was interrupted by a shout from the other side of the yard: "Maisie! What's going on there? Who's this?"

Two men approached. Sparrow recognized one of them as Major Lee, the trainer he had seen through the binoculars. The other was a tall man in breeches and a knitted sweater, carrying a heavy whip. Remembering what Gertie had told him, Sparrow guessed that this must be Hogg, Lee's assistant, the man who had taken her to the orphanage.

"See to the dog," Lee ordered the man.

"Satan!" Hogg shouted. "Kennel!" He cracked the whip, making a sound like a pistol shot. The dog cowered and slunk back to its home at the other end of its chain.

"Well?" Lee asked his daughter.

"This is Sparrow, Pa," she explained. "He wants to be a jockey."

"Does he now?" Lee laughed.

"I heard you might be needin' a new stable lad," Sparrow told him.

"That's more like it. D'you know much about horses, boy?"

"Not a lot. But I can learn – I'm a very quick learner."

Lee regarded him thoughtfully. His pointy face and cunning eyes reminded Sparrow of the foxes he sometimes saw rifling through the bins back in Baker Street. He turned to Hogg.

"What d'you think, Harry?" he asked.

"Well, I suppose he's the right size, guv'nor," his assistant replied grudgingly.

"You could try him out, Pa," Maisie suggested. "We do need another lad."

"Taken a shine to him, have you, my dear?" Her father smiled.

"I like the look of him, yes. I think he'll do."

"All right. Find him some kit. Those togs are no use here. I reckon young Tommie's stuff should fit him – and *he* won't be needing it any more. Harry, you can sort him out. Show him the ropes. I've got things to do."

And with that, Major Lee limped off, his stick clacking on the cobblestones.

"Well, my little cock Sparrow," Maisie said

brightly. "Looks like you're in luck. Come with me."

"Bring him back soon as he's ready," Hogg told her. "We've got no time to waste messing about."

As he turned away, Maisie pulled a face and poked her tongue out at his back. Then she led Sparrow off towards a black timber-clad barn. This took them past the dog, and Sparrow held back nervously.

"It's all right," she assured him. "You're with me. Anyway, you're one of us now."

She reached out and patted the dog's head. "Satan, this is Sparrow," she announced. "He's going to live with us."

The dog glared at Sparrow and let out a low grumble.

"Now, now!" Maisie admonished. "That's not very nice. Sparrow's a friend. *Friend*. Understand?"

She took Sparrow's hand and moved it towards the dog.

"Let him smell you," she instructed. "The back of your hand. That's it."

Satan sniffed, but still looked at the new boy suspiciously. Maisie reached into the pocket of her pinafore and produced a dog biscuit.

"Here," she said. "Give him this."

Swallowing hard, Sparrow held out the biscuit and the dog took it from him greedily, chomping it between its great teeth. Then, to Sparrow's surprise, Satan's tail twitched and briefly wagged.

"There. He likes you," declared Maisie approvingly. "You must be all right – he's a good judge of character is Satan."

Gertie returned to the caravan in the woods carrying an enamel can.

"Here you are," she said to Wiggins. "Straight from the spring. You won't never find water purer than that."

She fetched a mug from the caravan, poured some of the water into it and handed it over. Wiggins had been sitting on the caravan steps, thinking hard, ever since they had sent Sparrow off to the stables. But he had not come up with any answers yet. Without his special chair and hat and pipe, he found it harder to think and make plans.

"We gotta find out two things," he said finally, taking a swig of water. "Who and why. Who killed the lad, and why they did it. If we can find out why, then we can work out who."

"How do we do that, then?" asked Gertie.

"We'll have to see what Sparrow comes up with."

"I'm worried about Sparrow. Don't you think he might be in deadly danger?"

"He knows that. But it's the only way. I've warned him to be on his guard."

"He better be."

Maisie took Sparrow into the barn at the end of the yard, and led him past bales of hay and up a set of stone steps to the upper floor. Half a dozen narrow wooden beds were lined up along one wall, each with a small cupboard beside it. In the middle of the room stood a large table, with a long bench on either side and a pile of tin plates stacked on top.

"That was poor Tommie's," Maisie said,

pointing to the bed at the end of the row. "So now it'll be yours. And you can keep your stuff in here."

She opened the cupboard alongside the bed. It held some clothes and a few odds and ends – a riding crop, a couple of dog-eared books, a writing pad and a stub of pencil, a used paint-brush with bristles clogged with white paint, a pocket knife and a photograph that Sparrow guessed was probably of Tommie's mother.

"You'll have to keep this tidy," Maisie told him. "Harry Hogg used to be a sergeant in the army and he likes everything to be spick and span."

She took out a pair of riding breeches, a sweater and a flat cap and threw them on the bed.

"Put these on. Go on," she said, turning her back, "I won't look."

Sparrow took off his trousers and pulled on the breeches. "It's OK," he said as he fastened the buttons. "You can turn round now."

"Let's have a look. Yes, they'll do. Hello, what's that?"

Sparrow looked down and saw a white splodge on one leg, among the stains of mud and old horse manure.

"Looks like paint," he said, fingering it. "It's quite dry."

"Fancy that. I didn't think poor Tommie ever painted anything."

"What happened to him?" Sparrow asked, trying to sound innocent.

"Tommie? He got done in."

"How d'you mean, 'done in'?"

"Bashed over the head. Murdered."

Sparrow tried to look shocked, as if this was the first he'd heard of it.

"What – in here?" he asked, looking around the room anxiously.

"No, course not. Up in the woods. Tommie liked to go walking up there when he had a bit of time off. '

"That's awful. Did they catch the killer?"

"It was some Irish tinker," said Maisie. "He was camping out up there."

"Why would he want to kill Tommie?" said Sparrow.

"We reckon the lad caught him spying on the gallops, timing the horses. Most likely for some crooked bookie."

"Bookie?"

"Bookmaker. Somebody that takes bets on races. The 'book' is the list of runners – horses, that is – and the odds on each one winning. So if a horse is given odds of ten to one, say, that means if you bet a pound on it and it wins, the bookie has to give you ten pounds, as well as your own money back."

"But if it loses, he keeps your pound, right?"

"Right – as well as all the money that's been bet on the other horses that didn't win. So you see, it's worth a lot of money to a bookie to know which horses have the best chance of winning."

"And if he can time 'em on the gallops, he'll know which one's runnin' fastest?"

"You've got it. That's why we keep it secret. The bookies have to work out what odds to offer on each horse in a race. The one most people think will win is called the favourite, and it'll have the shortest odds – two to one, say. So if you bet a pound you'll win two. A horse that nobody fancies is called an outsider and it'll have the longest odds – maybe even a hundred to one."

Sparrow's mouth fell open at the thought. "So you get a hundred quid for every pound you bet! Wow! You could make a fortune."

Maisie laughed. "Or lose one. Outsiders hardly ever win – that's why they're outsiders. Come on now, that's enough jawing. Let's get you started."

As Sparrow and Maisie came out of the barn, the other stable lads were trooping back into the yard. They had finished giving the horses their morning exercise and had put them out to pasture in the paddock. Now they were hungry and eager for breakfast before starting the rest of the day's work. The smell of frying bacon and eggs wafted across the yard, and Sparrow's mouth started to water.

Hogg was standing in the yard, waiting for the lads, and he addressed them like the army sergeant he had once been.

"Now then, you 'orrible creatures. Line up and pin back your lugholes!"

The five lads stopped and stood facing him, trying not to stare at Sparrow.

"This puny specimen goes by the name of Sparrow – that's right, 'Sparrow'. Like the dickie bird."

Some of the lads sniggered. One, the biggest, called out "Tweet tweet!" and the others burst out laughing and made other bird noises. Sparrow just grinned back at them to show he was not upset or afraid. Maisie, standing off to the side, smiled indulgently and shook her head.

"All right, all right," Hogg shouted. "That's enough of that. Sparrow's joining us in place of Tommie, God rest his soul. He's never worked in a stables before, so it's down to you lot to show him what's what."

He pointed at the tallest of them. "Fred," he said, "you're head lad, so you're in charge of teaching him. I don't suppose he can ride. Can you ride, Birdie?"

"No, sir," Sparrow answered. "Never been on a horse."

"Right, Fred. Soon as you've had your brekker and finished mucking out, you can give him his first lesson. Put him on that little skewbald pony. That way he won't have so far to fall when he comes off."

Sparrow swallowed hard. The skewbald pony must be Gertie's Patch, so at least he would have some connection with his friends and not feel quite so alone. But the idea of falling off a horse, even if it was only a small one, was pretty scary. And when he thought of trying to ride the big, powerful animals that he had seen on the gallops that morning, his legs felt like they were turning to jelly.

Sparrow's fears were forgotten for the moment, however, when the smell of frying bacon grew even stronger as the kitchen door to the trainer's house was opened. A plump middle-aged woman wearing a long apron and holding a brass hand-bell stood in the doorway.

"Breakfast!" she shouted, ringing the bell furiously. "Come and get it!"

The five lads stampeded towards the door, leaving Sparrow standing alone. "Not hungry, Birdie?" Hogg asked.

Sparrow nodded cautiously. He was ravenous, but not sure what to do.

"Well, what are you waiting for? Get in there, lad."

* * *

The breakfast was the best Sparrow had ever eaten. It tasted even better than it smelt. The other lads were too busy eating to talk, stuffing food into their mouths and mopping up the greasy juices and egg yolk with hunks of bread. Sparrow did the same, not looking up until he had finished and was washing it down with a mug of sweet tea. When he did, he found the woman looking down at him approvingly.

"That's what I like to see," she said with a smile. "A boy with a good appetite. And who are you?"

"This is Birdie," said Fred. "New lad, just started. In place of Tommie."

"Ah, poor Tommie. I shall miss him."

"Yeah. We all will."

"My name's Sparrow."

"Is it, now? And mine's Cook, 'cos that's what I do."

"But everybody calls her Cookie," explained Fred. He pointed out the other lads, one by one. "That's Alfie, that's Ginger – don't ask me why – and Charlie and Jim." They each looked up and nodded at Sparrow, greeting him with a "Wotcha" or a grin and a wink.

When he had introduced them all, Fred stood up and clapped his hands. "Right, lads. Back to work!"

Over the next few hours Sparrow worked harder than he had ever done in his entire life. To start with, Fred took him into one of the loose boxes and pointed to the deep layer of straw covering the floor. It was full of manure.

"Cor!" Sparrow exclaimed, wrinkling up his nose. "Pongs a bit, don't it?"

"You'll get used to it," Fred said. He thrust a fork at Sparrow. "That's your first job. Muckin' out. Clear this lot, load it into a barrow and take it to the muckheap over there. Then come back for another load."

The big wooden wheelbarrow was heavy even when it was empty. By the time it was filled with wet straw and manure, Sparrow could hardly lift the handles.

"Come on! Chop chop! Get a move on!" Fred shouted. "Think you're on your holidays, do you?"

The rest of the lads paused in their work to watch.

"Whoa there, hang on a minute," Fred called with a wicked grin. "I reckon there's room for a bit more."

With that, he tossed another forkful onto the loaded barrow, which was now piled so high it was hard to balance, or to see over. Sparrow just managed to lift the handles and stagger forwards, but he had only taken a few steps before the whole thing fell over. All the dirty straw tipped out, scattering across the cobbles. Fred roared with laughter and the other lads joined in.

"You'd better get that lot cleared up afore the guv'nor sees it," Fred told Sparrow. "He can't abide a messy yard."

RIDING LESSONS

When the mucking out was finished and the loose boxes had been washed down, the lads had to fetch bales of hay and fill the racks on the back walls. It was hard work, but not as heavy as the wet straw. And, unlike the straw, it smelt sweet and fresh. The only problem for Sparrow was that it made him sneeze.

"You got a cold, Birdie?" Fred asked.

"No. Somethin's ticklin' my nose."

"I'll tickle your nose with my fist if you give my horse a cold," Fred said fiercely.

"Which is your horse?" Sparrow asked.

"The champion, of course. Silver Star. Best horse in the country. I'm lookin' after him now that Tommie's gone."

"Was he Tommie's horse, then?"

"Tommie should never've had him. Never!" Fred's face contorted into an expression of hate. "I'm the head lad. I should have the best horse. 'Stead of which I got that useless Blackie and they gave Silver Star to their precious Tommie."

"Didn't you like Tommie, then?" ventured Sparrow.

"He was a crawler," replied Fred. "Suckin' up to everybody. A right goody-goody."

"Oh. Right." Sparrow made a mental note. This was something else to report to Wiggins.

"Well, can't stand here gassin' all day. Got to get you a saddle for your first lesson."

Fred led Sparrow across the yard and into another barn. "This is the tack room," he told him. It smelt strongly of leather and polish and other things that Sparrow did not recognize. Hanging on hooks and pegs around the walls were reins and harnesses and saddles. Fred selected one of the saddles, lifted it down from its peg and thrust it at his charge.

"It don't look very big," Sparrow said, remembering the comfortable saddles he had seen on horses in the London streets. This one seemed quite tiny.

"It's a racin' saddle," said Fred. "That's what we use here, so you might as well get used to it from the start. Come on."

Fred marched off out of the yard and Sparrow trailed after him, carrying the saddle. When they reached the paddock, he saw six racehorses quietly cropping the grass. They looked elegant and powerful, with their long legs and strong muscles.

"Which one's Silver Star?" asked Sparrow.

"There." Fred pointed to two horses that were grazing a bit away from the others.

"Which? They both look the same to me."

"Do they?" Fred smiled. "Look harder. Look at the hooves."

"Oh, I see. That one looks like he's got little white socks on his front legs."

"That all?"

As Sparrow watched, the horse with the white socks raised its head and he could see its face for the first time. There was a diamond-shaped white mark between its eyes.

"There," said Fred. "See the star on his forehead?"

"Oh yeah. I get it. Silver Star. So that one must be Blackie," he said, pointing to the other horse. It had no white markings and its coat was black all over.

"Well done. His proper name's Black Velvet, but that's a bit of a mouthful, so we call him Blackie."

"Is that the one you used to look after?" asked Sparrow.

"Still do. I look after both of 'em now. So you're gonna help me. And I don't want anybody else touchin' either of 'em. OK?"

"OK."

"Don't forget that. Just you and me. Anybody else goes near 'em, you tell me."

Fred moved into the next paddock, where Gertie's Patch was grazing alongside two ordinary ponies that were obviously not racehorses. As they entered the paddock, Patch ambled over to greet them.

"Wotcha, Patch," Sparrow said, patting her neck.

"How d'you know her name?" asked Fred.

Sparrow gulped. Had he given himself away? He thought hard for a moment, then answered, trying to sound cheerful. "Er, I don't. I just thought ... all them different colours ... like patchwork."

Fred looked at him suspiciously, but then shrugged and managed a tight smile.

"Yeah. I see what you mean. 'Patch' suits her. Well, come on. Get the saddle on her."

Sparrow heaved the saddle onto Patch's back and stared at the straps and stirrups with no idea what to do with any of them. Fred watched and waited as Sparrow tried to fit the saddle, getting into an ever-deeper muddle as he went on. Finally the older boy spoke.

"What a mess. You've got it on back to front for a start."

Sparrow lifted the saddle and turned it round, but everything was still in a hopeless tangle and he became more and more flustered and red-faced.

"Why don't you show him how it's done?" Maisie's voice came from behind them. She had arrived without them noticing.

Fred glowered at her, his eyes like burning coals.

"He'll learn better if he does it himself," he said.

"Not first time, he won't," Maisie retorted. "And why have you given him a racing saddle?"

"It's what he'll be usin'."

"Not while he's learning. It'll make it ten times harder. Or do you *want* him to keep falling off?" she asked.

Now Fred's face had turned bright scarlet. He did not look at Maisie, but glared angrily at Sparrow.

"He's gotta learn," he muttered.

"The hard way?"

"The hard way's the best," the head lad said gruffly. "Helps you remember things."

"Does it? I think it would be better if *I* taught young Sparrow to ride."

Fred fumed. "Mr Hogg told me to do it. What's he gonna say?"

"Leave Mr Hogg to me. I've got more time than you, anyway. Go on – off you go."

As Fred stomped off back to the stables, Maisie turned to Sparrow.

"Let's get you a proper saddle, shall we? Bring the pony round to the tack room. It's easier to take the horse to the saddle than carry the saddle to the horse."

Sparrow spent the rest of the afternoon learning to ride Patch. He fell off several times but always climbed back on, determined to master it. Maisie was a good teacher: patient and kind, but firm. By teatime she had Sparrow trotting round the paddock. He was bruised all over and had a very sore bottom and aching thighs, but he could stay on and was actually starting to enjoy it. He was even learning to rise and fall in the saddle, like a real rider, instead of bouncing up and down like a sack of potatoes. But it was still hard work and he was glad when Maisie decided it was time to stop.

"You've done really well," she praised him. "I think you might be a natural."

Sparrow thanked her, glowing with pride. He had become so engrossed in the lesson that he had quite forgotten why he was there. He was brought back to earth with a bump, however, when they arrived back at the main house. Standing outside was a familiar black carriage. The coachman hopped down to open the door as its owner came out of the house with Major Lee.

Maisie stopped, and Sparrow saw that she had gone pale.

"What's up?" he asked her.

"That man," she whispered.

"D'you know who he is?"

"No. But I don't like him. And neither does my father."

"What's he doin' with him, then?"

Maisie gave a sigh. "I wish I knew. I'm sure it's something bad, but Pa won't talk about it."

Sparrow said nothing. He would have loved to tell her who Moriarty was and to warn her against him. But that would have meant admitting why he was there and what he was doing. He tried to hide behind Maisie and Patch as the arch-criminal descended the steps from the house and climbed into his carriage. Moriarty was so clever that he might well have recognized Sparrow as being one of the Baker Street Boys, and that would never do.

"What are you doing?" Maisie asked him.

"I don't like the look of him either," Sparrow said quickly. "He's creepy."

"Yes, he is. Come on, let's put this saddle away and get Patch back in the paddock."

As the carriage started up and turned to go, Fred came out of one of the loose boxes. Sparrow was surprised to see him touch his cap at Moriarty. Was he simply being polite? Sparrow didn't think that very likely – so far, the head lad had not struck him as a very polite person. Or did he know Moriarty? What did it mean? Sparrow didn't know, but it was something else to report to Wiggins. He was sure to know what it meant.

Sparrow's bottom was so sore from his long afternoon of riding that he had to eat his tea standing up. The other lads laughed at this, but it was in good fun – they all remembered how they had felt when they started riding. When they had eaten, their last job of the day was to collect the horses from the paddock and shut them in for the night. Fred told Sparrow to fetch

Blackie while he led in Silver Star. It was not hard. Both horses were well behaved and knew the routine – they went into their own stalls without being told and settled down quietly.

Fred inspected each horse carefully, looking it over and running his hands over its flanks and legs.

"Got to be sure they ain't done theirselves no damage durin' the day," he explained to Sparrow. "We're sendin' 'em both out on Thursday."

"Where to?" asked Sparrow.

"The races, of course. They're both runnin' in the Prince's Cup at Ally Pally. That's one of the biggest races in the calendar."

"Ally Pally?"

"Short for Alexandra Palace. It's near Muswell Hill in north London. So for once we ain't got far to travel."

"Will you be goin' with 'em?"

"Course I will," said Fred, and Sparrow could hear the pride in his voice. "I'm ridin' Blackie."

"You mean in the race?" exclaimed Sparrow. "Like a real jockey?"

"Yeah, that's right. I'll be a jockey full time

soon. When I've done a few more rides and had a few wins."

"Must be great to ride a winner," Sparrow said, trying to imagine what it would be like.

"Best feelin' in the whole wide world," Fred replied, his eyes shining. "When you come into the final straight and everybody's goin' flat out and the crowd's shoutin' and cheerin'... Magic!"

"How many winners have you rode so far?"

Fred looked uncomfortable.

"I've only just started," he said. "I'm still learnin'."

Sparrow nodded sympathetically. "P'raps you'll win on Thursday," he said brightly.

Fred stared at him warily and did not answer at once. Then he gave a little cough, as though he had something in his throat.

"What, on Blackie?" he said at last. "No chance."

"Why ain't you ridin' Star, then?"

"Star's a top horse," Fred explained. "So he gets a top jockey. Willie Carforth, last year's champion."

"Cor. He's bound to win, then. Eh?"

"Yeah. Bound to."

"I bet you wish you was ridin' Silver Star."

"One of these days I will," the head lad replied with a small smile. "*I'm* gonna be champion jockey. Just you wait and see."

It had been a long, hard day and Sparrow was worn out. He ached all over and it wasn't just his bottom and legs that hurt. His hands were sore too, from using the big fork to muck out and pushing the heavy barrow. As soon as he reached the hayloft dormitory he collapsed onto his bed, and before he knew it he was fast asleep.

He did not sleep for long, though. After a few minutes he was woken by a loud voice in his ear.

"Oi, Birdie! Tweet tweet! Wakey, wakey!" Fred shouted. "Ain't time for you to go to sleep."

"Go 'way!" Sparrow groaned. He opened one eye. Fred was leaning over him, shaking him by the shoulders. The other lads were all gathered round his bed, looking down at him and grinning.

"You're a new lad," Fred went on. "And when we gets a new lad, he has to be initiated."

"Eh? Inishywot?"

"You got to do somethin'. It's like a forfeit. Maybe you could take a dip in the water trough in the yard."

The other lads laughed and made shivering noises. Sparrow was suddenly wide awake.

"Or eat a plate of horse manure – Cookie said you got a good appetite…"

The lads burst into raucous laughter.

"Tell you what," said Fred, "why don't you do a turn, eh?"

"A turn?"

"Yeah, you know – a dance or somethin'. Make us laugh. Or how about singin' a song? A little birdie should be good at that."

Sparrow brightened up. That was something he *could* do.

"OK," he said, trying to look reluctant. "I'll sing you a song."

There was a disappointed groan from the other lads.

"Right," said Fred. "Up on the table! And if we don't like it, you can still eat horse muck."

The table was cleared in an instant, and the lads watched expectantly as Sparrow climbed onto it. He took a deep breath, then started one of his favourites from the music hall:

> *Our parlour wanted paperin', and Pa*
> *   said it was waste*
> *To call a paperhanger in, and so he*
> *   made some paste.*
> *He bought some rolls of paper,*
> *Got a ladder and a brush*
> *And with my mummy's nightgown on,*
> *At it he made a rush.*

He paused for effect, then launched into the chorus, complete with actions.

> *When Father papered the parlour*
> *You couldn't see Pa for paste.*
> *Dabbin' it here, dabbin' it there,*
> *Paste and paper everywhere,*
> *Mother was stuck to the ceilin',*
> *The children stuck to the floor,*
> *I've never seen a bloomin' family,*
> *So "stuck up" before!*

The lads stared at him in amazement and burst into laughter as he started a little comic dance along the table. Sparrow went on to sing half a dozen more verses, each one funnier than the last, and got the others to join in the choruses after he had called out "All together now!". When he finished, they cheered and clapped and yelled for more.

"Where d'you learn to do that?" Ginger asked.

"I was a call boy in the Imperial Music Hall for a bit," said Sparrow. "I got to see all the stars. Learnt their acts, watchin' 'em every night."

Fred was the only one who hadn't laughed during Sparrow's song and dance. "Why ain't you still there?" he asked sourly.

"I, er, fell out with Mr Trump, the manager," Sparrow said.

"Kicked you out, did he?"

"Sort of, yeah."

"What for?" asked Fred, his eyes narrowing. "Thievin'?"

"No! Nothin' like that," Sparrow cried indignantly.

"I bet I know," said Jim. "I bet you was too cheeky. Ain't that right?"

Sparrow shrugged. "Might be."

"Well, make sure you don't give Harry Hogg no cheek," Jim told him. "He'll have you out on your ear in no time."

"Won't stand for it at all," Alfie agreed.

The other lads nodded seriously.

"Never mind all that," said Ginger. "Have you got any more songs?"

"Yeah! More! More!" they all cried.

"What shall I do? I know... You'll like this one."

Sparrow jumped down from the table, opened his cupboard and grabbed the paintbrush that he remembered seeing earlier. The lads helped him back onto the table, and he began.

"This is a little number called 'Slap Dab'," he announced. "Are you ready? Right, here we go, then..."

And with that he proceeded to sing a song about a man whitewashing his garden fence, all the time doing a comic dance with the brush, singing faster and faster until the words tumbled into each other and he quite ran out of breath.

The lads enjoyed this even more than the first

one, and they all clapped and cheered and whistled. All except Fred, who just stood there looking furious. He snatched the brush from Sparrow's hand and thrust it under his nose.

"Where did you get this?" he demanded.

"Out of Tommie's cupboard. Why?"

"What d'you think you're playin' at?"

"I ain't playin' at nothin'," Sparrow protested, taken aback. "Just singin' a song."

Fred stared at him for a long time, trying to decide whether or not to believe him. "I got my eye on you," he snapped at last. "And don't you forget it."

NIGHT IN THE DARK WOODS

It had grown dark in the woods. Wiggins and Gertie sat waiting on the steps of the caravan, hoping that Sparrow would come soon, but there was no sign of him. Wiggins began to worry. After all, a lad had been murdered in these very woods only a few days before. He knew he had sent Sparrow into danger, but the Boys were Gertie's father's only hope – if they could not prove he was innocent, he would be hanged.

As the shadows grew longer, the wood became more and more spooky. The ancient trees, with their weird twisted shapes, seemed threatening. Some seemed to have gruesome faces, others arms that could reach out and grab you, and it was easy to imagine that they were moving. There was a loud clatter, followed by an eerie wailing, like a ghost, and Wiggins almost jumped out of his skin. He was not used to the countryside, and the night-time sounds were strange to him.

"What was that?" he asked Gertie, trying not to let his nerves show.

"Sure and it was only an old owl," Gertie reassured him. "They hunt at night, y'know. A lot of creatures do."

"And so do a lot of criminals," Wiggins retorted.

"I dare say Sparrow can't get away. He'll come when he can."

"Yeah, course he will. He's a good lad."

They sat in silence for another minute or two, then Wiggins got to his feet.

"I don't like it, Gertie," he said. "I'm going to look for him."

Gertie stood up. "I'll come with you," she said. "I don't fancy stoppin' here on my lonesome."

They closed the caravan door and set off together along the winding path through the trees. By now the moon was coming out, so they could just about see where they were going. But it cast another set of shadows, pitch-black holes in which anything could be hiding. Wiggins and Gertie were both glad when they came to the edge of the woods.

"Careful now," said Wiggins. "We don't want to be seen."

Looking down the hill, they could see the stables below. There was a light shining in one of the bedrooms in the house, but the rest of the buildings were all dark.

"Looks like everybody's asleep," said Gertie.

"Yeah – including Sparrow."

In fact, Sparrow was not asleep. He was so weary after his long, hard day that it was a struggle to keep his eyes open, but he knew that if he let them close he would go straight to sleep, and he would not be able to report to Wiggins. At last, when he was sure the other lads were all asleep, he slipped quietly out of bed and arranged his pillow under the blanket so that it looked as though he was still sleeping. Then he pulled his breeches on over his shirt and tiptoed across the room. To his relief, no one stirred.

Sparrow crept down the stairs into the barn and out into the yard. He was stopped by a deep warning growl. He froze. If the dog started barking it would surely wake everybody.

"Quiet, Satan," he whispered urgently. "Good boy. It's me. Sparrow. Remember me?"

The dark shape of the dog emerged from its kennel and crossed the yard towards him, still growling. Sparrow realized with a start that it was not chained up. It must be let loose in the yard at night, free to attack any intruders. With no chain to hold it back, it would reach him quite easily before he could get to the gate. Sparrow thought of those huge teeth and his own teeth chattered with fear.

"Good boy, Satan," he repeated. "Friend. Good boy." He held out his hand, palm down, as Maisie had shown him earlier. The dog sniffed at it, wagged its tail briefly, then sat down, its eyes fixed on him.

"Sorry, Satan," Sparrow said. "I haven't got a biscuit for you this time."

At the word "biscuit" the dog wagged its tail again. Ordering it to stay, Sparrow backed carefully away until he felt the gate behind him, then he turned and climbed over it. The dog watched him with a disappointed look on its face.

"Next time, eh?" said Sparrow, then scooted off.

Up on the hill, Wiggins and Gertie were about to return to the caravan when they saw Sparrow in the moonlight, climbing the gate.

"It's OK," said Gertie. "Here he comes."

"Phew," Wiggins replied, "just in time! I was starting to think something had happened to him. Wait a minute, though. Who's that?"

He pointed to the house. In the lit bedroom window, a figure moved. Wiggins and Gertie couldn't see who it was, but someone was looking out, watching Sparrow as he hurried towards the woods.

Wiggins listened very carefully as Sparrow told him everything about his day.

"Well done," he said when Sparrow had finished. "You've given me plenty to think about."

"But what does it all mean?" Gertie asked.

"Dunno yet. I wish I'd got my special chair and Mr Holmes's old hat and pipe. I s'pose I'll have to manage without 'em."

"We need to know what Moriarty's up to," said Gertie.

"And why Fred got so upset when you sang those songs," Wiggins added.

"And why he won't let nobody else go near Silver Star and Blackie," said Sparrow.

"Yeah, and a whole lot of other things as well," agreed Wiggins.

"Most of all," said Gertie, "we still don't know who killed Tommie."

"Or why. You gotta go back there, Sparrow, and carry on keeping your eyes peeled for anything that might give us a clue."

Sparrow nodded and set off down the hill, dragging himself back to the stables. His legs felt so heavy that he could hardly put one foot in front of the other, and all he could think about was his bed. As he arrived back in the yard, he was far too tired to notice someone looking out of a bedroom window. But as he passed the loose boxes, he did notice a light seeping out under the closed door of Silver Star's box. Someone was in there with the horse. Sparrow could hear low voices inside, but they were speaking so quietly he could not hear what was being said, or who was saying it. He crept closer to peep through the crack in the door, when it began to open. He just had time to hide around the corner before two people came out. One was Fred, carrying a lantern. The other was Hogg, wiping his hands on a piece of rag.

"It'll be dry by morning," Sparrow heard Hogg say. "Just keep everybody away from them. How's the new lad?"

"You don't have to fret about him," Fred replied with a chuckle. "He don't know nothin', and I'm workin' him so hard he don't have time to think."

"Good. Make sure you keep it that way."

"I will. No problem."

"Now, you'd better get back to your pit or you'll be good for nothing in the morning. Go on – off with you."

While the head lad made his way back upstairs, Sparrow had to wait where he was, giving Fred chance to fall asleep before he dared to follow. Then he crept back to his own bed and was dreaming even before his head hit the pillow.

Wiggins and Gertie made their way back to the caravan safely. All seemed quiet and peaceful now, and they were soon fast asleep on their bunks. After only a little while, however, Gertie was woken by a noise from outside. She sat up and peered through the window, then gently shook Wiggins's shoulder.

"Wake up," she whispered, putting a hand over his mouth to keep him quiet. "There's somebody outside."

Wiggins blinked up at her. "You sure it ain't another owl?" he mumbled sleepily.

"I ain't never seen a owl carryin' a bull's-eye lantern," she said.

Wiggins was awake in a flash. He looked through the window. Gertie was right, there was someone out there – and he or she was making their way towards the caravan. The door creaked open and the dark figure of a man appeared in the doorway. The beam from his bull's-eye lantern swung around the inside of the caravan, and lit up Wiggins and Gertie. The man let out a yell, stepped back – and fell down the steps. Wiggins leapt up and charged through the door after him. The man was lying flat where he had fallen. His lantern lay on the ground beside him, its beam pointing up into the sky. Wiggins threw himself on top of him, pinning him down, while Gertie sat on his legs.

To their surprise, the man showed no signs of fighting them off. Instead, he raised his arms protectively in front of his face.

"Don't hurt me," he whimpered pitifully. "Please don't hurt me."

"What d'you want?" Wiggins demanded, trying to sound fierce and strong.

"I don't mean no harm. I only want what's mine."

"Who are you?"

"My name's Sneyd. Sam Sneyd."

"Ha!" Gertie cried. "You're Slippery Sam!"

The man turned pink. "I believe some people do call me that," he said huffily.

"Hmm," said Wiggins. "You might as well get up."

He climbed off the man's chest and nodded to Gertie to free his legs. Sneyd sat up, checking himself to make sure nothing was broken or damaged, then scrambled unsteadily to his feet. Gertie picked up his lantern and shone the light on him so they could see him properly. He was a short man, no taller than Wiggins, and just as wiry. He brushed himself down, then smoothed back his greasy black hair and ran a finger along his thin moustache.

"I s'pose you've come for your spyglasses, stopwatch and notebook," Wiggins said in his best Sherlock Holmes manner.

"How d'you know...?" Sneyd began.

"They must be worth a lot of money," Wiggins continued. "But not as much as you hoped to make betting on Silver Star."

"Silver Star's a dead cert," said Sneyd. "But I need to be quite sure before I bet all I've got on him. If I do and he don't win, I'll have lost everything."

"Well don't bet, then," said Gertie.

"I have to. It's the only way. I got debts, see? I owe some bad people a lot of money."

"What happens if you don't pay 'em?" Wiggins asked.

"It could be very nasty," replied Sneyd with a shiver. "They might even kill me."

"Like somebody killed young Tommie, you mean?" said Wiggins sharply.

Sneyd paused for a moment. "I heard about that. Terrible."

"What did you hear? What d'you know about it?"

Sneyd shook his head so hard, Wiggins thought it might fall off. Or at least break his neck.

"Nothing. I don't know nothing about it. Honest."

"What about my da?" Gertie asked. "D'you know who set him up?"

"No. No, I don't. But I know he couldn't have done it," said Sneyd.

Wiggins and Gertie both leant forwards eagerly.

"How d'you know that?" Wiggins asked.

Sneyd ran his finger along his moustache

again. "Because he was with me the night it happened."

Wiggins turned to Gertie accusingly.

"I thought you said he was with you?" he cried.

Gertie looked sheepish. "Sure and he might have slipped out of the caravan while I was asleep," she admitted.

"Without waking you?"

"He can move very quiet when he wants to," she said.

"That's true," Sneyd agreed. "Quiet as a mouse. I'm sure he could walk on eggshells without breaking them."

Wiggins thought for a moment, wondering what Mr Holmes would have said next. Eventually he turned back to Sneyd.

"So, Mr Sneyd. You say Patrick was with you that night?"

"Yes."

"That's very convenient for you, ain't it?"

"How d'you mean, convenient?" asked the man nervously.

"Well, if Patrick was with you, that gives you an alibi as well, don't it?"

"I … I … I don't need an alibi," Sneyd stammered. "Nobody says I did it."

"But you was in this wood the night Tommie was murdered?" Wiggins persisted.

"I was, yes."

"And you didn't see nobody else?"

"I might have done. But I can't be sure. I didn't see Tommie, either."

"So you say, Mr Sneyd. So you say…"

"Yes, I do say."

"Thank you," Wiggins said, taking hold of the lapels of his jacket like a lawyer interrogating a witness in court. "I've only got one more question for now."

"What's that?"

"What was Tommie doing in the woods? Where was he going?"

Sneyd looked confused. His mouth opened and closed but no sound came out. Gertie stepped in.

"I dare say he was comin' to see us."

"Did he usually come at that time of night?" Wiggins asked her.

"No," she said. "He usually come earlier in

the evenin', while it was still light."

"So why was he coming then?" he pressed.
"That's another thing we gotta find out. And
when we do, we'll know who killed him."

A BLACK-AND-WHITE CASE

Sparrow was so weary the next morning that the other lads had to tip him out of bed before he could wake up. He lay on the hard floor, trying to collect his thoughts, wondering why every bone and muscle in his body ached. Ginger and Jim had to stuff his legs into his breeches, then pull them up. Alfie and Charlie stuck his feet into his boots and all four of them hauled him upright and helped him to climb unsteadily down the stairs.

"Come on, Sparrow," Ginger urged. "You better not let Hogg see you like this. He'll have you runnin' round the yard till you drop."

It was barely light in the yard, but Fred had already washed himself in the big stone water trough. He took one look at Sparrow's bleary eyes and laughed.

"What's this, Birdie? Can't wake up? Soon put that right. Come here."

He grabbed Sparrow by the neck, shoved his head into the water and held it under. It was bitterly cold and Sparrow struggled to escape, desperately holding his breath. Just as he thought he was going to drown, Fred finally let go. Sparrow surfaced, gasping for air.

"There you are, Birdie." Fred guffawed. "You awake now?"

Sparrow nodded, speechless.

"Say thank you, then, like a good lad."

"Thank you," Sparrow spluttered.

"Thank you, Fred," corrected the head lad.

"Thank you, Fred," Sparrow repeated.

"That's more like it." Fred clapped his hands loudly. "Right, let's get these boxes opened up. Give the hosses some air."

The lads moved quickly along the row of boxes. As they opened the stable doors, the horses stuck their heads out, snorting a welcome to the day. To Sparrow's surprise, when he opened Silver Star's door it was Blackie's face that appeared. He turned to find Fred looking at him.

"Why is Blackie in Star's box?" he asked.

Fred made an angry gesture. "That stupid Hogg," he said. "He must have put 'em back wrong last night."

"Hogg?"

"Yeah. We thought Star might have a bit of a strain coming on," Fred explained, "so we took both of 'em out to give 'em a rub down. Can't be too careful with the big race so close."

"Last night?"

"After you lot had turned in. Can't you smell the liniment?"

Sparrow sniffed. He had already noticed a powerful medical smell.

"Pooh," he said. "I wondered what the pong was."

"Horse liniment. You'll soon get used to that, workin' in a stables. We might even give *you* a rub down with some – ease your aches and pains," said Fred with a malicious smirk. "So, Birdie, better open up next door and see if Star's in there."

Sure enough, when they opened Blackie's door the horse that appeared had the familiar white star on its nose. Sparrow reached out to stroke it, but Fred grabbed his arm.

"Don't do that," he said fiercely. "He don't like having his face touched. Listen, don't say nothin' about this to nobody. Old Hoggy wouldn't want anybody to know he'd been careless with Star, right?"

"Right."

"Come on then, let's get the bridles and saddles from the tack room. Then you can start muckin' out while the rest of us ride 'em out to the gallops."

In the woods, Wiggins was startled from his sleep by a deafening cacophony. It sounded as though every bird in the world was singing its heart out to greet the day.

"What the dickens is that all about?" he asked.

"Sure and that's the dawn chorus." Gertie laughed. "All the little birds wakin' up and shoutin', 'Good mornin', everybody, I'm still here.'"

"Do they have to make so much noise about it?" moaned Slippery Sam, who had stayed at the caravan overnight so that he could see for himself the racehorses working on the gallops.

The three of them shared the last of the bread and cheese that the kind Mrs Gorman had given them before they left London. Then they picked up the binoculars, stopwatch and notebook from the cupboard and made their way to the edge of the woods. There, they concealed themselves among the bushes, making sure they could still see all the way to the gallops. They did not have to wait long before the string of horses appeared. Fred was at the front, riding Silver Star and leading Blackie on a long rein. The other lads followed on their horses. Major Lee and Hogg rode alongside them and took up their positions.

The three spies watched from the bushes as the horses were put through their morning exercise routine, warming up gradually until at last they were ready to start galloping flat out. Sam leant forwards eagerly and raised the binoculars to his eyes. This was what he had come for.

"Steady, now," Wiggins warned him. "Stay back. The sun's getting up and we don't want it reflecting off the glasses. That would give us away and we'd be done for."

Sam looked at him with interest.

"You're a clever one, ain't you? Where d'you learn it all?"

"I've got a good teacher." Wiggins grinned.

"Who's that, then?"

"Mr Sherlock Holmes."

"What, the great detective?" asked Sneyd.

"One and the same. We're his irregulars, the Baker Street Boys. Me and Gertie and another five. There's seven of us, all told."

"Well I never. Where are the others, then?"

"Four are back at our HQ in London, waiting for instructions."

"That only makes six," Sam pointed out.

"Correct. We got one working inside the stables."

"Phew!" Sam stared at Wiggins in open-mouthed admiration. "How d'you manage that?" he exclaimed.

Wiggins gave him a mysterious smile and tapped the side of his nose.

"Did Mr Holmes fix it?"

"No," Wiggins answered. "Mr Holmes is away in Germany. We're doing this ourselves."

"What, trying to catch a murderer?" said Sam in disbelief.

"That's right," Gertie said firmly. "And we will."

"How are you going to do that?"

"You'll see. We're gonna get my da off – especially now we've got you to help us. When you go to the police and tell Inspector Lestrade…"

Suddenly Sam looked shifty and even more nervous than usual.

"Ah, now wait a minute—"

"Hang on," Wiggins cut him off. "They're starting, look." He pointed to the horses. Major Lee was holding up a white handkerchief. When he brought it down, Fred kicked Silver Star into action. The horse leapt forwards. Holding the glasses to his eyes with one hand, Sam clicked his stopwatch with the other as the horse passed the first post. He followed it round until it passed the second post at the end of the course, when he clicked again. As Fred pulled the horse up and turned to canter back to the start, Sam licked the point of his pencil and wrote down the timing in his notebook.

Down below, Major Lee consulted his

stopwatch and spoke briefly to Hogg, before signalling to Fred. Fred changed horses, then galloped round on Blackie, and once more the major and Sam both timed him. Sam carefully wrote down the result but looked puzzled. He scratched his head and looked at the stopwatch again. Then he turned back the pages of the notebook.

"That's funny," he said.

"What is?" asked Wiggins.

"Black Velvet ran faster than Silver Star."

"Sure and that's not possible," said Gertie. "Everybody knows Star's faster than Blackie."

"Not today he ain't," said Slippery Sam. "According to this little book, that's the first time Blackie's beat him. Ever."

"I see you've made friends with Satan," Maisie said.

Sparrow was busy mucking out Silver Star's loose box, and the dog was lying on the ground near by, lazily watching him.

"He's all right when you get to know him," Sparrow replied.

"Or when he gets to know you. I told you he's a good judge of character. Can you manage that on your own?" Maisie added, seeing him struggle to lift the heavy load.

"I need to get it finished before Fred and the others get back."

"Well, don't wear yourself out too much. We've got your next lesson when you've finished here."

Sparrow grinned and groaned at the same time. He didn't know whether he was looking forward to his lesson, or dreading it. He liked the idea of learning to ride, and enjoyed being taught by Maisie, but he knew it was going to be painful. He lifted another fork load of soiled straw and put it into the barrow. Suddenly something in it caught his eye and he leant over to inspect it more closely.

"Hello," he said, picking up a handful of straw. "What's that?"

Maisie peered over his shoulder.

"Looks like paint," she said. "Black paint."

"Yeah," said Sparrow, fingering it thoughtfully. "It's dripped onto the straw, see? As if somebody's spilt it."

"Funny," Maisie remarked. "Nobody's been doing any painting lately. Not as far as I know."

Sparrow shrugged, trying not to show the excitement he felt inside. This could be an important clue. He could hardly wait for Maisie to leave so that he could look for the next piece of evidence. He was beginning to put things together and if he was right, he would have something very interesting to tell Wiggins that night.

As soon as Maisie moved away, Sparrow hurried into the next box. Kneeling down, he inspected the straw inside the door. Just as he had suspected, he found more drips of paint. But this time, they were white.

"You reeker!" he cried. "Gotcha!"

For the rest of that day, Sparrow worked hard. He finished mucking out Silver Star and Blackie, fetched and carried for Fred, cleaned and polished saddles and harnesses. He endured another riding lesson on Patch and earnt praise from Maisie for his progress. The daily routine of life in the yard carried on around him and nothing seemed unusual or odd. A few tradesmen came and went, delivering food for both people and horses. The postman rode up, bringing the mail. A traveller called at the house, trying to sell mops and dusters. An old knife-grinder on a specially built bicycle set up his equipment in one corner of the yard and sat pedalling hard to sharpen knives, scissors and tools. He spoke kindly to Sparrow and showed him how his grindstone worked, which was interesting, but nothing to report to Wiggins.

By teatime Sparrow was worn out again. His last job of the day was to help bring the horses in for the night, and as he did so he paid careful attention to Silver Star and Blackie to see what they would do. Sure enough, the all-black horse headed for Silver Star's usual box and the other started to go into Blackie's. Sparrow said nothing as Fred quickly stepped in and steered them into the correct stalls, but made a note of it all to tell Wiggins. By now he was quite certain what was going on, but he still wasn't sure why.

After tea – a nourishing stew that was almost as good as Queenie's – the lads were free to do as they pleased. Most of them had hobbies.

Ginger was whittling a piece of wood with a sharp penknife, carving the figure of a horse; Alfie was making a model boat; Charlie was drawing a picture of horses in a race. Jim was trying, unsuccessfully, to juggle three rubber balls. Sparrow tried to give him a few tips, which he had learnt from his Chinese friends in the music hall, but Jim didn't want his help.

"What you gonna do with yourself, Birdie?" Fred asked.

"Dunno," Sparrow answered. "Thought I might do a bit of explorin'. Find my way around, y'know."

"Well, don't go too far."

"No," Ginger warned. "Don't forget what happened to poor Tommie."

"You'll be all right," Charlie told him. "They got the murderer locked up in jail."

Sparrow was quite puffed out by the steep climb up the hill to the woods. In fact, it was only the thought of telling the others his exciting discoveries that kept him going, and by the time he reached the caravan he was looking forward to sitting down. As he came through the trees into the clearing, however, he saw that Wiggins and Gertie were not alone. He stopped and quickly ducked back into the trees. Was that strange man a friend or foe, he wondered. Fortunately he did not have to decide. Gertie spotted him and ran to greet him.

"Sparrow!" she cried. "You're OK!"

"I'm fine," he answered. "Who's that?"

"This is Slippery Sam," Gertie replied. "The one my da was workin' for."

"Sneyd," the man corrected. "My name's Sam Sneyd."

"He's helping us," Wiggins added. "He's the one what give Gertie's dad the stopwatch and spyglasses."

"Er, *lent* them," Sam said quickly.

"Are you a bookie?" Sparrow asked him.

Sam looked at him sharply, wondering how much he knew. "Yeah, sort of."

"He knows my da's innocent," Gertie told Sparrow excitedly. "And he's gonna help us prove it."

"T'rific!" said Sparrow, lowering himself to the ground with a groan.

"Sparrow?" Wiggins sounded worried. "You OK?"

"Just a bit tired," he said wearily.

Gertie fetched a mug, filled it with water and handed it to him.

"Here," she said, "have a drink. It'll do you good."

Sparrow thanked her and drained it in one go. Gertie was right. It did make him feel better.

"Now then," said Wiggins, "what you got for us? You seen anything?"

Sparrow grinned, took a deep breath and started to tell his friends everything that had happened and what he had seen and heard. They listened with great interest. When he had finished, Wiggins stood up and clapped.

"Brilliant!" he proclaimed. "I couldn't have done better myself. Sparrow, you deserve a medal."

Gertie joined in Wiggins's applause. "That explains what happened on the gallops this mornin'," she exclaimed.

"What happened?" asked Sparrow.

"Blackie ran faster than Silver Star."

"Yeah. Only it weren't Blackie – it was Silver Star painted to look like Blackie!" cried Wiggins.

"A bit of black paint on Silver Star, and a bit of white paint on Blackie. That's all it takes. The perfect disguise for both of 'em."

"But what I don't get is why," Sparrow said. "What's it all for?"

"Money," Wiggins said. "Lots and lots of money."

"That's right," agreed Sam. "They're doing a ringer."

"What's a ringer?"

"A ringer is a lookalike," explained their new friend. "A horse that's swapped for another horse which looks similar. So everybody thinks they're betting on one horse, but it's really a different animal. It might be better, or it might be worse. It doesn't matter as long as you know which it is."

"'Cept in this case, it's two ringers. Side by side," said Wiggins.

"Well I never! The crafty so-and-sos," said Gertie.

"The thing is, what we gonna do about it?" Sparrow wanted to know.

Sam stood up, rubbing his hands with glee. "I know what I'm gonna do. I'm gonna get back to London, first thing in the morning. Get some bets on."

"You can't do that," Sparrow protested. "That'd be cheatin'."

"I know. But it'd make me rich." Sam grinned.

"Not if we told the coppers what was going on," said Wiggins.

"You wouldn't." Sam's face fell. "Would you?"

"Course we would," said Gertie. "If you wanna win, you gotta do it fair and square."

"But I could pay off all my debts! I'd be free from those bad men that are after me."

Wiggins shook his head. "Sorry, Sam. Mr Holmes would never forgive me."

"He doesn't have to find out," retorted Sam.

"Mr Holmes always finds out," said Sparrow. "That's why he's the world's greatest detective."

"Just my luck," Sam moaned. "What are you gonna do, then?"

"I dunno," said Wiggins. "I'll have to think about it. It ain't what we're here for, after all. Sparrow, you better get back. Act normal, keep your eyes and ears open and don't say nothing to nobody about what we've found out."

HORSE THIEVES

The light was fading as Sparrow made his way back through the woods. When he came out of the trees, he could see the yard below. The stables and the house looked peaceful, with all the doors to the loose boxes closed for the night. He pictured the horses resting quietly, and wished he was already in his own bed. Fortunately it was all downhill now, so the going was easy and he even broke into a trot on the slope. He was nearly home when he heard the distant grinding of wheels on gravel, and a moment later he saw a carriage approaching. It was getting quite dark and he could not see it very clearly, but he was pretty sure it was Moriarty's.

As the carriage neared the yard, Satan started barking furiously. The front door of the house opened and Major Lee looked out to see what was going on. Recognizing the carriage, he ordered the dog to be quiet and strode across to the gate. The carriage door opened and the major spoke briefly to the person inside, then climbed in.

Sparrow bent low and crept along the fence until he reached the carriage. Crouching by the back wheels to keep out of sight of the coachman, he could just hear what was being said within. There were two voices. One was the major's. The other was Moriarty's familiar rasping hiss. "There must be no mistakes this time. No more nosy stable lads to be got rid of."

"There won't be," the major replied. "We tested both horses this morning. No one suspected a thing."

"Excellent. If you want to keep your stables, you had better make sure it stays that way. Now, listen carefully. We must take no chances. When the race has been won, you will bring the horse back here and get rid of it."

"Get rid…? What d'you mean?"

"You know what I mean. The evidence must be destroyed. And that horse is the evidence."

There was silence for a moment, then Major

Lee spoke again. His voice was choking. "Destroy Silver Star? I couldn't."

"You must. Or risk losing everything. You must kill him."

Wiggins, Gertie and Slippery Sam were just about to head towards the caravan for the night when they were disturbed by the sound of someone crashing through the undergrowth in the woods. They were surprised to see Sparrow bursting into the clearing, gasping for breath.

"Sparrow!" Gertie cried. "What's up?"

"Are you all right?" Wiggins asked anxiously. "Is somebody after you? Have they hurt you?"

Sparrow shook his head but couldn't speak. He sank to the ground. Although he had been tired, he had managed to summon up enough energy to scramble back up the hill. But now he was exhausted.

"Got to…" he panted, "got to tell…"

"Take your time," said Wiggins. "Catch your breath."

They waited until Sparrow could breathe enough to speak.

"Now," said Wiggins, "what are you trying to tell us?"

"They're gonna kill Silver Star."

"Who are?"

"Moriarty and the major. I heard 'em talkin' about it. Soon as he's won the Prince's Cup."

"Disguised as Blackie, you mean?" said Wiggins.

"Yes. Once he's won, they're gonna bring him back here and shoot him."

"Why?" Gertie asked.

"To destroy the evidence, the professor said. He told the major that the horse is the evidence, and he's got to be got rid of."

"But won't everybody know there's summat fishy goin' on?" asked Gertie.

"No. They're gonna say he had an accident and broke his leg."

Sam nodded slowly. "The crafty beggars. Everybody knows that when a racehorse breaks a leg it has to be put down. It'll never race again."

"I see," said Wiggins. "So they shoot it, bury it and nobody's any the wiser."

"But what about Blackie?" Gertie asked. "He's evidence as well. They wouldn't dare kill both of them at the same time. That really would look fishy."

"Right," said Sparrow. "They're gonna put him out to grass somewhere miles away. Once he's been cleaned up he'll look like any other black horse with no special markin'. Then a bit later, after it's all gone quiet, they'll get rid of him, too."

"That's a cryin' shame," cried Gertie. "Those beautiful animals! I can't bear the thought of it."

"We gotta do something, that's for sure," Wiggins declared. "But what?"

"Hang on," said Sparrow. "I ain't finished tellin' you yet."

"What?"

"That wasn't all Moriarty said. He said he didn't want no mistakes this time. 'No more nosy stable lads to be got rid of.'"

The other three stared at Sparrow, open-mouthed.

"That's it!" yelled Wiggins. "It was *them*! And now we know why!"

Gertie looked thoughtful. "So Tommie found out what they was up to. He must've caught 'em practisin' or somethin'. They'd have needed to try the paint before they did it for real, and he must've seen 'em and guessed the rest."

"And they had to shut him up afore he told anybody," Wiggins concluded.

"Who was he gonna tell?" asked Sparrow.

Wiggins paced back and forth across the clearing, thinking hard and muttering to himself. The others watched and waited until, at last, his face cleared.

"Gertie's dad, of course," he said. "He was gonna tell Gertie's dad!"

"Yes!" Gertie cried. "*That's* what he was doin' up here at that time of night."

"Well," said Sam, "now you know all that, you can just tell the coppers. You don't need me any more. I can go home."

"Oh no you don't," said Wiggins. "We gotta prove Patrick didn't do the murder. You gotta give him his alibi."

"Oh. Yeah." Sam looked downcast. He didn't like the idea of talking to the police.

"And we gotta provide the evidence," added Wiggins.

"What's that?"

"The horse, of course. Silver Star with his marks painted out so he looks like Blackie. We gotta get Inspector Lestrade to take a look at him afore the race. That's the only way we can stop 'em shooting him."

"We ain't got much time, then," said Sparrow.

"When's the race?" asked Gertie.

"Prince's Cup?" said Sam. "Ally Pally, 3.30, Thursday."

"Thursday?" Wiggins exclaimed. "That's tomorrow!"

"Oh, lawks," muttered Sparrow gloomily. "We ain't got no time at all. We'll never get the inspector out here by then."

"Well, that's that, then," said Sam, getting to his feet. "We might as well give up and go home."

"Hang on." Wiggins held up a hand to stop him. "We're the Baker Street Boys. We don't give up."

"What you gonna do, then?"

"Only one thing we can do. If the inspector can't come to the horse, we'll have to take the horse to the inspector."

The others all stared at Wiggins as they realized what he was saying.

"How d'you think you're gonna do that, then?" Sam asked at last.

"Simple," Wiggins replied. "We take him out of the stables tonight, while everybody's asleep."

"You mean *steal* him?" Sam looked aghast. "You're gonna steal a racehorse?"

"Not steal him. Rescue him," corrected Wiggins.

"D'you really *want* to go to prison?"

"We ain't the ones what'll be goin' to prison," said Sparrow. "It's the major and Hogg and Fred what'll get locked up, when the coppers find out what they've been up to."

The three Boys and Sam had to wait until everyone in the stables was in bed. By the time the last light had gone out it felt like the middle of the night, but they dared not move until they were sure everybody was asleep. Eventually they crept towards the yard. Clouds were floating in front of the moon, so it was not as bright as it had been the night before, but there was still enough light for them to see where they were going. Sam carried his bull's-eye lantern with the front closed.

"What are you going to do about that dog?"

Sam whispered nervously. "If it starts barking…"

"It won't," Sparrow told him. "Just leave the dog to me. I'll go first."

He moved towards the gate and called very quietly, "Satan! Satan!"

"Satan? What you on about?" hissed Gertie.

"Shh! It's the dog's name. Here, boy. It's me, Sparrow."

The dog ambled towards him, wagging its tail. Sparrow patted it gently on the head.

"There. It's OK, boy. These are my friends." Satan growled. "Friends … friends, Satan. OK?"

He beckoned to the others. Wiggins and Gertie slipped in through the gate after him, but Sam held back.

"You can stay here," Wiggins told him. "On guard. Keep cave for us in case anybody comes. OK? Just give me your lantern."

Sam nodded gratefully and handed over his bull's-eye lantern, then watched as the three Boys tiptoed across the yard. Sparrow opened the door to Blackie's loose box and stroked the horse's neck as he had been taught, whispering calmly to reassure it.

"You quite sure you got the right hoss, Sparrow?" Wiggins asked.

"Yes. This is Silver Star all right."

"Ain't he just beautiful?" Gertie cooed.

"Come on," Wiggins urged. "We ain't got time to stand about admiring him."

"He's got his head collar on already," Sparrow said, "so all we need is the reins to lead him by... Should be hangin' up over here. Just shine the light."

Wiggins opened the lantern and shone it on the wall. The reins were hanging by the door. Sparrow took them and clipped them onto the horse.

"That's it," he said. "Let's go."

"Go where?" a new voice demanded. It was Maisie, standing in the doorway. She was wearing a dressing gown over her nightdress. And she was holding a shotgun.

"Who are you and what d'you think you're doing?" she asked. "Why are you trying to steal Blackie?"

"We ain't stealin' him," Sparrow answered, his heart thumping. "We're savin' him."

"*Sparrow?* Is that you? Who are these people?"

"They're my friends," said Sparrow.

Maisie stared at the Boys. She pointed at Gertie accusingly. "I've seen you before," she said.

"You might have," Gertie retorted. "Me and my da have been campin' in the woods up there."

"Now I know who you are. Your da ... er, your father murdered Tommie!"

"No, he never," declared Gertie with a sniff. "He's innocent."

"And we're gonna prove it," Sparrow said. "That's what we're doin' here."

"You can tell that to the police," Maisie replied sternly. "After you've explained yourselves to my father."

The Boys' hearts sank. It seemed that their plan was doomed. When an owl hooted somewhere in the darkness, it sounded as though it was laughing at them.

Wiggins stepped forward. "No!" he said urgently. "Please. Don't say anything to him till you've heard what we've got to tell you."

"I don't understand," said Maisie. "Who are you?"

"Arnold Wiggins," Wiggins introduced himself, "captain of the Baker Street Boys."

"Baker Street...?"

"Special assistants to Mr Sherlock Holmes, the world-famous detective. And this is Gertie O'Grady. She's one of us and all."

"And Sparrow?" Maisie asked, looking confused.

"Yes," said Wiggins. "He's one of us as well, working undercover. So you can put the gun down, if you please. We ain't robbers. We're detectives."

Maisie considered for a moment, looking hard at each of them, then lowered the shotgun and stood it against the wall. "It isn't loaded, anyway," she said. "Now, what's this all about? Where were you going with Blackie?"

"To show him to our friend Inspector Lestrade at Scotland Yard. Only this ain't Blackie, is it?"

"What are you talking about?" the girl asked in bewilderment.

"This ain't Blackie, it's Silver Star," Wiggins asserted.

Maisie gave a little laugh. "Don't be silly," she said. "If this is Star, where are his markings?"

"Painted out," Sparrow told her. "That's what that paint was, on the straw. Remember? Black in

Star's box, white in Blackie's?"

Maisie put her hands to her face, her eyes as wide and round as saucers.

"Oh my goodness." She gasped. "That's terrible!"

"Yes," said Wiggins. "And you're saying you don't know nothing about it?"

"Of course not," she replied indignantly. "I wouldn't do such an awful thing. Who would?"

"Your pa, and Mr Hogg," said Gertie.

"And Fred," Sparrow added. "They're all in it together."

"All in what?"

"They're doing a ringer," explained Wiggins. "Have you ever heard of a ringer?"

"I … I think so, yes. But it's cheating. My father wouldn't do that!"

Maisie shook her head in bewilderment. Wiggins took hold of the lapels of his jacket, as he had seen Mr Holmes do.

"It's my belief," he said in his most serious voice, "that your pa has got himself in the grip of an evil man called Professor Moriarty."

"How do you know all this?"

"You learn a lot when you work for Sherlock

Holmes. Moriarty is a master criminal. We've crossed swords with him before. Your father ain't the first to fall into his clutches."

"But what makes you think he has?" asked Maisie.

"'Cos we've seen Moriarty with him," Wiggins told her.

"We seen him at the gallops. And he was here tonight," said Sparrow. "I heard 'em talkin'. They was plottin' to do away with Silver Star after he's won the Prince's Cup tomorrow."

"No!" she protested. "My pa would never do anything to harm Star. Never."

"The professor told him he's got to," Sparrow went on. "He's gotta kill Star and destroy the evidence. Or he'll lose the stables and everythin'."

"That's why we gotta get Silver Star outta here," said Wiggins. "Tonight."

"But where can you take him that's safe?"

"We'll take him to London. To Scotland Yard."

"It's a long walk to London," Maisie said. "I don't think Sparrow will make it. He's proper worn out."

"I'll be all right," Sparrow protested. "I can't stop here, anyhow."

"No," agreed Wiggins, "not with Star gone. They'll soon twig what you've been up to. And we don't want another Tommie."

"He could stay in the caravan," Gertie suggested.

"First place they'd look," Wiggins said. "They'd find him in no time."

"Patch!" Maisie cried, clapping her hands.

"What?"

"You can take Patch. She's Gertie's anyway. Sparrow could ride her."

"We could take it in turns," Sparrow said.

"What about Star?" Gertie asked.

"Much too dangerous. Sparrow couldn't ride Star."

"No, but I could. I can ride anythin'."

Maisie looked doubtful.

"Don't worry. He'll be safe with me."

"Safer than if he stayed here," added Wiggins.

Maisie thought about it and decided Wiggins was right.

"OK. You'll need two saddles. Come on. Quiet as mice, now!"

They crept round to the tack room, taking care not to make a sound. Across the yard, Sam was waiting impatiently by the gate. Satan sat near by, never taking his eyes off him. When Sam saw Maisie leading the three Boys out of the stable, he quite forgot about the dog and started towards them. Quick as a flash, Satan was on his feet. His deep growl turned into a snarl as he leapt towards Sam and buried his teeth in Sam's backside. Sam clapped his hand over his mouth to stifle a yelp, then jumped back through the gate to get it between himself and Satan.

"Who's that?" Maisie said, spinning around.

"It's all right," Wiggins said. "That's Sam. He's with us."

"Another detective?" she asked.

"No, he ain't," Gertie told her. "He's a bookie. But he's helpin' us."

"I hope he's OK. Looked like Satan bit him on the bum."

"Yeah." Sparrow grinned. "You said that dog was a good judge of character."

Maisie soon had a saddle on Silver Star and they led him out of his box and across the yard, making as little noise as they could. Satan's teeth had not gone through the thick cloth of Sam's trousers, so he was just bruised. The five of them made their way over to the paddock, where Patch was grazing alone. When she heard Gertie's voice, the skewbald pony whinnied with delight and cantered across to nuzzle and butt her in greeting. She seemed pleased to see Sparrow, too, and stood happily while he helped Maisie saddle her and climbed onto her back.

"You'd better get going," Maisie said. "Good luck!"

"What're you gonna do?" Wiggins asked her.

"I don't know yet. We don't want anybody coming after you, so I shan't say anything till I know Star's safe. Then – well, we'll have to see. At any rate, I'll be going to Ally Pally for the Prince's Cup tomorrow."

"Don't worry about Star. We'll take good care of him," Gertie promised as she mounted the racehorse. "Nobody's gonna hurt him while the Baker Street Boys are on the case."

A Night Ride

There was no sign of life as the little procession made its way along the dark lane from the racing stables. Sparrow was dozing in the comfortable saddle on Patch's back, just managing to stay awake. Gertie was thrilled by the power of Silver Star. She could feel his muscles rippling as he moved. Secretly she wished that the journey would never end so that she could go on riding this wonderful creature for ever.

Wiggins, however, knowing how far they had to walk, couldn't wait for the journey to end. He was leading Patch by the reins while Slippery Sam trudged alongside him in silence. But as they passed the pub in the village near the stables, Sam suddenly turned off.

"Oi," Wiggins called. "Where you going?"

"I left my bike here," Sam explained. "I'm going to collect it."

He hurried round the back of the pub and came back a minute later wheeling a bicycle.

"You never said nothing about having a bike," Wiggins accused him.

"Didn't I? Oh well, I got it now, so I don't have to walk back to London after all. I might see you there. Cheerio."

With that, Sam swung his leg over the crossbar and set off down the road, pedalling furiously as he disappeared into the distance.

"I'll get after him," said Gertie. "Star'll catch him up in no time."

Wiggins stopped her. "No," he said. "Let him go."

"But I need him to give my da his alibi!"

"Don't worry. I'm sure the coppers know him very well. They'll soon find him."

The streets of north London were deserted as the three Boys passed through. They had been travelling all night, and dawn was breaking as they reached the top of Highgate Hill. A fat policeman, patrolling his lonely beat, stepped out into the road and held up his hand to stop them.

"Whoa!" he ordered, producing a lantern from under his cape and shining it on their faces in the dim early morning light. "Where d'you think you're going? And where did you get those horses?"

"That one's mine," Gertie told him. "She belongs to me and my da."

"Oh yes? And what about the other one? That's a fine-looking animal for a scruffy bunch of ragamuffins to have in their possession. It looks like a proper classy racehorse to me."

"It is," said Wiggins. "We're taking him to Scotland Yard."

"Don't try to get clever with me, my lad," said the policeman.

"It's true," Sparrow piped up. "We're goin' to see Inspector Lestrade. D'you know him?"

"No, I don't. Inspector Lestrade's a very high-up detective."

"*We* know him," said Wiggins. "And he knows us. We're the famous Baker Street Boys."

"Famous who? Never heard of 'em."

"We work for Mr Sherlock Holmes," Wiggins added.

"A likely tale! You'd best come along with me to the station. See if we can find out who this valuable beast belongs to and where you've stolen him from."

"We didn't steal him," insisted Sparrow. "We rescued him."

"Well, I'm sure the owner will be pleased to get him back."

"No! You can't give him back to the major," Sparrow blurted out. "He's gonna put him down!"

"The major, eh?" the policeman said. "Now which major would that be, I wonder?"

"Sparrow!" Wiggins shouted. "Shut up!"

"Oh, Lor'!" Sparrow groaned. "Sorry."

Wiggins looked at the policeman. He was fat and had big flat feet in his heavy boots. It only took Wiggins two seconds to decide what to do.

"Run for it!" he cried. "He'll never catch us!"

Sparrow and Gertie kicked their heels hard into their horses' sides. Wiggins slapped Patch on the rump. She jumped forwards and lumbered into action, with Sparrow clinging on for dear life. Gertie crouched forward over Star's neck as he took off in an electric burst of speed, as if it was the start of a race. Wiggins ran as fast as he could behind Patch. The fat policeman ran after them for a little way but quickly gave up. He pulled out his whistle and tried to blow it, but he was too out of breath. In any case, there was no one near by to hear. He stood puffing and panting as the Boys and their horses soon disappeared out of sight.

Further down the road, Gertie slowed Silver Star to a walk and pulled into a little park, where she let the horse graze on the grass while she waited for the others. They arrived a few minutes later, with Wiggins sitting on Patch's back behind Sparrow.

"We can rest here for a few minutes," Wiggins said after they had all dismounted. "But then we'll have to be on our way again. It won't take the coppers long to work out who the major is. And they know who we are, too, so they might come looking for us around Baker Street. We'll have to hide Star somewhere till we can get to Lestrade."

"We can't hide him in HQ," said Gertie. "He'd never get down all them steps."

"We need a stable," said Sparrow.

"Yes," Wiggins agreed. "But where are we gonna find...? Wait a minute... Shh!"

"What?"

"Listen!" They heard the sound of hooves echoing through the quiet street. "There ain't many people out at this time of the morning, is there?"

"Only market folk," Gertie said.

Wiggins slapped himself on the forehead. "And milkmen!" he cried. "Of course!"

They hurried out of the park just in time to see a pony and trap approaching at a steady trot. In the driving seat was a familiar figure wearing a peaked cap and striped apron.

"Mr Gorman!" Gertie called out. "Mr Gorman! Stop!"

The milkman pulled up and stared at them in surprise.

"Oh my goodness," he said. "Not you lot again. And what's that?" He stood up in his trap and peered into the park. "It looks like a racehorse."

"It is," said Wiggins. "It's Silver Star."

Mr Gorman shook his head and laughed. "Oh no it's not," he said. "I can see that from here. Silver Star's famous for the white blaze on his face. That's where he gets his name from."

"It's a long story…" began Wiggins.

"I can't stop now. I'm on my way to collect the day's milk from the farm, and I can't keep my customers waiting."

"We'll tell you all about it when you get back. In the meantime, we need somewhere to keep him safe and out of sight. Can we put him in your stable? In the empty stall next to Betsy's?"

"Well, I don't know about that…" said the milkman reluctantly.

"Please?" Gertie pleaded.

"It's a matter of life and death," Sparrow added. "Honest."

"Is it now?" Mr Gorman pushed back his cap and scratched his head while he thought it over. "Oh, all right. Just till I've finished my morning round."

Queenie was cutting slices of stale bread for Beaver and Shiner in the secret cellar that was the Baker Street Boys' HQ. Rosie was not yet back from Covent Garden flower market. Suddenly there was the clatter of footsteps on the stairs and Wiggins, Gertie and Sparrow burst in through the door.

"T'rific," said Wiggins. "Brekker. I'm starving. Been walking all night."

He grabbed a piece of bread, threw himself down in his special chair and started chewing hungrily.

"Well?" demanded Queenie. "Ain't you gonna tell us?"

"Yeah," said Beaver. "Where you been? What you been doin'? We want to hear everythin'!"

"I learnt to ride," said Sparrow. "I rode Patch all the way home. Didn't fall off once."

"Who's Patch?" Queenie asked.

"You find the murderer?" asked Shiner.

"Not yet," said Gertie. "But we got my da an ali-baba."

"Alibi," Wiggins corrected her.

"That's right. Proves he didn't do it."

"And we stopped a big crime, and rescued a racehorse," Sparrow went on.

"Blimey." Beaver gave a low whistle. "You ain't half been busy."

"Yeah, and we ain't finished yet," Wiggins said. "We gotta talk to Inspector Lestrade and give him our evidence so he can wrap it all up."

"Where's your evidence?" Queenie asked.

"In Mr Gorman's stable."

"Eh?"

Wiggins smiled at the look on her face. "It's a horse," he explained.

"A famous racehorse called Silver Star," Gertie added. "Moriarty was makin' the trainer do a ringer with him."

"Moriarty?" Shiner exclaimed. "Don't tell me he's mixed up in all this."

"He is," Sparrow said. "He's lyin' low and pullin' the strings, like he always does. I seen him with the major, and I heard him talkin' 'bout doin' away with Star, to get rid of the evidence."

"And that'd be just terrible," Gertie said. "We had to do somethin' to stop it."

"So we pinched him and brought him home," finished Sparrow.

Beaver still looked puzzled. "What's a ringer?" he asked.

Before Sparrow could answer, the door opened and Rosie bustled in, carrying her trayful of flowers. She gave a shriek of pleasure when she saw Wiggins, Sparrow and Gertie.

"Oh, thank goodness you're back." She plonked her tray down. "It's good to see you safe and sound. What's that horse doin' outside?"

"Horse?" Queenie dashed to the door, followed by Shiner and Beaver. Patch was standing in the courtyard, waiting patiently, nibbling at a clump of weeds.

"That ain't no racehorse," scoffed Shiner. "That's a gypsy nag."

"No it's not," said Gertie. "That's Patch. And she's mine."

"Well, where's your racehorse, then?"

"I told you," Wiggins said. "Safe out of sight in Mr Gorman's stable. We gotta go and see Dr Watson and get him to fetch the inspector."

When Billy opened the door of 221b Baker Street, Wiggins did not wait to be announced. Instead he pushed past the startled pageboy and charged up the stairs, followed by Sparrow and Gertie. This time Dr Watson had not even started his breakfast. He was in the middle of shaving, and half of his face was covered in lather.

"What on earth…?" he began, waving his open razor in mid-air.

"Sorry, Doc," Wiggins said. "You gotta come quick. It's urgent."

"Has there been an accident? Is someone ill?"

"No, no. Nothing like that. But the big race is this afternoon, so we ain't got much time if we're gonna save Star and Blackie."

The doctor looked completely bewildered.

"Hold on," he said, lowering his razor. "I don't understand. You'll have to explain."

"We got evidence of a murder and a swindle and we need Inspector Lestrade to come and see it. Afore the races this afternoon."

"Whatever your evidence is, can't you take it to him?"

"No. It's too big."

"And anyway, he won't listen to us," Sparrow joined in. "But he'll listen to you."

"I see. At least I think I… What is it?"

"A horse," said Wiggins

"Ah… What sort of horse?"

"A racehorse."

"Oh dear. And where exactly is this racehorse?"

"Just round the corner. In the stable behind Mr Gorman's dairy."

"It ain't just any old racehorse," Gertie added. "It's Silver Star."

"Silver…?" The doctor sat down heavily in a chair. "Silver Star's the most famous racehorse in the country! And you've got him in a milkman's shop?"

"That's right," said Wiggins, enjoying the doctor's look of astonishment. "D'you know anything about racing?"

"I enjoy a little flutter – a small bet – every now and then," admitted the doctor. "Silver Star's the hot favourite to win the Prince's Cup, I believe."

"Exac'ly. Only the horse what's gonna run as Silver Star ain't what he's s'posed to be."

Dr Watson frowned.

"Are you saying that it's…?"

"A ringer. Yes, Doctor. They're gonna cheat people out of thousands and thousands of pounds if we don't stop 'em."

"And poor Tommie found out about it," said Gertie.

"The stable lad who was murdered?"

"Yeah. That's why he was done away with. To stop him telling."

"So my da had nothin' to do with it, y'see. They set him up because he's a tinker and we was camped in the woods."

The doctor got to his feet. "The fiends!" he declared indignantly. "We must go to Scotland Yard at once."

He wiped the lather from his face, threw open the door to the landing and shouted to Billy to find a cab while he finished getting dressed.

As they trundled across London in the cab, the three friends told Dr Watson all that had happened.

"You've done extremely well," he told them after listening with great interest to their adventures. "I'm most impressed – and Mr Holmes will be too when he returns from Germany."

"We've still got a few loose ends to tie up," admitted Wiggins.

"Well, perhaps Inspector Lestrade will be able to help you with them. We'll see what he has to say."

The cab stopped outside Scotland Yard. The doctor paid the driver, then led the Boys to the entrance.

"We've come to see Inspector Lestrade," he told the policeman guarding the door. "My young friends have some important information to impart to him."

"I'm sorry, sir," the policeman said. "I'm afraid it will have to wait. The inspector's not in today."

"Can you tell us where we might find him? It's rather urgent."

"I'm afraid you can't, sir. He's on special duty."

"Oh dear. That's most inconvenient," said the doctor. "Can't you get a message to him?"

"Sorry, sir, but he's taking care of His Royal Highness the Prince of Wales."

"Would that be at Ally Pally?" Wiggins asked.

"How d'you know that?" the policeman said, surprised.

"The prince will be presentin' the prize for the big race," said Sparrow.

"The Prince's Cup," Gertie chipped in.

"That's right," the policeman said. "So you see, Inspector Lestrade won't be able to talk to you. You'll have to wait till tomorrow. Likely he'll be here then."

"Likely it'll be too late then," Wiggins answered gloomily. He turned to the others. "We've failed. Come on, we might as well get back to Baker Street."

Wiggins threw himself down into his chair. His chin drooped onto his chest and he looked weary and depressed.

"D'you want your hat and pipe?" Queenie asked. "To help you think?"

"No use," he replied. "There ain't enough time for that. We've missed our chance."

The other Boys were all gathered round in HQ, waiting for their captain to tell them what to do. But he was too tired to have any bright ideas.

"There ain't no way we can get Lestrade round here afore the race," Wiggins moaned.

"Well," said Queenie after a moment's silence, "strikes me there's only one thing we can do."

"Give up?" suggested Shiner.

"Don't say that," Queenie snapped at him. "I don't ever want to hear you talk like that. We're the Baker Street Boys and we never give up."

The others nodded in agreement, but no one had any other suggestions.

"Go on then, clever clogs," Shiner snapped back at his sister. "What we gonna do?"

"It's obvious, ain't it?"

"What is?"

"Like we said before – if we can't get the inspector to come to the horse, we gotta take the horse to the inspector. Right?"

"Right!" the rest of the Boys chorused.

"We know where Lestrade is," said Sparrow. "We just gotta get Star into Ally Pally."

A RACE AGAINST THE CLOCK

Mr Gorman steered his pony and trap into the yard behind his shop, glad to have finished his round for the day. He was uneasy about having a famous racehorse hidden in his stable. He had been happy to help the Baker Street Boys but couldn't help worrying what the police would say when they found out. His horse, Betsy, stopped suddenly.

"Oh my word," Mr Gorman said. "What are you lot doing here?"

All seven Baker Street Boys were waiting for him in the yard. Silver Star was looking out of the stable door, watching them with interest, wondering where he was and what on earth was going on.

"We've come to collect Star," Gertie said.

"And to say thank you for havin' him," Queenie added politely.

"What are you going to do with him now?" Mr Gorman asked.

"We're gonna take him to the races," said Sparrow.

"What, at Ally Pally?"

"That's right," said Wiggins.

Mr Gorman shook his head and pulled a long face.

"They'll never let you in," he said. "They'll take the horse off you and lock you up."

"Not if they don't know who he is," said Shiner.

"Well, I suppose they'll think he's Black Velvet," Mr Gorman agreed, "but that won't make any difference. He'll still be a stolen racehorse."

"No he won't," said Wiggins. "I got a plan. But we need your help."

"Oh no." Mr Gorman groaned. "What is it this time?"

"We need to borrow your milk cart."

The milkman listened, astonished, as Wiggins told him his plan. They would unhitch Betsy from the trap and put Star in her place. Wiggins and

Gertie would drive the trap to the service entrance at the rear of Alexandra Palace, with Wiggins wearing Mr Gorman's cap and apron. Wiggins would tell the gatekeeper that they were delivering milk to the restaurant, and they would be let in. Once they were safely inside, they could unhitch Star, find the inspector and reveal everything.

When Wiggins had finished, there was a long silence. The Boys waited anxiously to see what Mr Gorman would say. To their dismay, he slowly shook his head.

"No," he said, "I won't let Wiggins and Gertie drive my trap to Ally Pally."

"Oh please, Mr Gorman," they pleaded all together. "*Please*. We'll take good care of it, we promise. It's the only way—"

Mr Gorman held up his hand to stop them.

"No," he said firmly, interrupting them. "I won't lend you my cart … I'll drive you there myself. That way you'll be sure to get in."

The Boys cheered. "Oh thank you," said Rosie, throwing her arms around him and giving him a kiss on the cheek.

"Anyway," Mr Gorman went on with a smile,

"my cap would be far too big for Wiggins. He'd look silly in it. Now listen," he added, serious now. "I can only take two of you at the most. There's no room for more, and besides, I couldn't roll up at the gate with half a dozen rapscallions on my cart. It wouldn't look right. So what are the rest of you going to do?"

For a moment the Boys looked crestfallen. Then Queenie spoke up.

"Dr Watson!" she cried. "He'll take us. We can go with him."

"Good thinking, Queenie," said Wiggins. "Gertie can go with Mr Gorman, 'cos Star knows her. And I'll go too, 'cos it's my plan."

"What about me?" asked Sparrow.

"You need to be with the doctor, 'cos you know who the villains are. You can keep your eyes peeled for the major and Hoggy."

"And Fred," said Sparrow.

"And Moriarty," added Beaver. "Don't forget Moriarty."

"Right," said Wiggins. "All of you'd better get round to 221b straight away. We'll see you at Ally Pally."

"Extra milk delivery for the restaurant," Mr Gorman told the gatekeeper. "They say they're running short."

"I'm not surprised," said the gateman. "We got a good crowd here today."

"All come to see Silver Star win the Prince's Cup, I expect," said Wiggins.

"You're right, young 'un. Must be thousands and thousands of pounds bet on him."

"Be funny if he lost," Wiggins couldn't resist adding cheekily.

"Ha! Funny for the bookies right enough." The gatekeeper grinned. "They'd like that – make a fortune, they would. Go on, you'd best get going if you want to deliver your milk and see the big race. Not long now till the off."

Mr Gorman twitched the reins and told Star to walk on, and they moved forward towards an enormous building that had to be the exhibition and entertainment centre, Alexandra Palace. The racecourse was further down the hill on the other side of the building, and when they turned the corner they could see it below them. The racetrack itself was a long loop of bright green turf with a white rail alongside it. Crowds of people lined the rail, jostling for a better view. Their excited shouts grew louder and louder, turning into cheers as a tight bunch of horses thundered past the winning post. Silver Star pricked up his ears and moved restlessly between the shafts of the milk cart, eager to be racing.

"Look!" Mr Gorman pointed to the centre of the grandstand that overlooked the finishing post. "There's the prince, in the royal box."

"Where?" Gertie asked. "Which one is he?"

"The fat one," said Mr Gorman. "With the pointy beard."

The prince stood in the centre of the crowded box surrounded by men in grey top hats and elegant women in silk dresses and large bonnets.

"And there's Inspector Lestrade," said Wiggins. "Can you see him?"

Lestrade was standing to one side, behind the prince.

"He's got his best uniform on," said Gertie. "He don't usually wear that, does he?"

"No. Must be 'cos he's on royal duty, protecting the prince."

"I don't know how you're going to get near him," said Mr Gorman. "He'll be sticking close to the prince, and the prince won't leave the royal box."

Wiggins scratched his head, then his face lit up.

"Oh yes he will," he said. "He's got to."

"When?"

"When he presents the cup to the winner."

"True," said Mr Gorman. "He'll have to go down to the winners' enclosure to do that."

"But how we gonna get Star in there?" asked Gertie.

"Simple," replied Wiggins with a broad grin. "He'll go in automatic when he's won the race."

"But how…?"

Wiggins pointed down the slope. "There's the others with Doctor Watson. They're looking for us."

"They're headin' for the stables area," said Gertie.

"That's where we gotta go too. Leave the cart

here, Mr Gorman, and unharness Star. We need to saddle him up quick."

"Right," said the milkman. "I've got his saddle and reins in the trap – I had to take 'em off him to get the harness on."

Gertie and Mr Gorman soon had Star unhitched and saddled.

"Now what do we do?" Gertie asked Wiggins.

"You get up on his back and ride him down to the stables, nice and easy. There's horses coming and going there all the time. Nobody'll take any notice of one more."

"I gotta horse! I gotta horse!" The cry came from a strange-looking Indian man with a black beard and a large turban, who stepped in front of the gang of Boys and held out a folded piece of paper to Dr Watson.

"What's he mean?" Rosie asked, puzzled. "Why does he say he's got a horse?"

"He's what they call a tipster," explained the doctor. "Offering to sell inside information on the best bets."

"Only one shilling for the best hot tip," the

man continued. "You want to know who's going to win the 3.30? I got it! Only a bob, that's all I'm asking, sir. One shilling."

"No, thank you," the doctor replied politely but firmly. He pushed past the man, who touched his turban in a salute. Queenie stared at him. There was something oddly familiar about the man, but she couldn't quite think what it was. Seeing her looking, the man winked heavily at her and touched a finger to his lips. Then he was gone.

A few steps further on they met another tipster – and this time there was no doubt about who he was.

"This is Slippery Sam, Doctor," said Sparrow.

"Sam Sneyd," Sam corrected with a frown. "At your service, sir."

"Ah, yes," said the doctor. "I've heard about you from my young friends here. You'd better come with us. We may have need of you."

"Er, I'm a bit busy right now…" Sam began, turning to run. Queenie gestured to Beaver and Shiner, who each grabbed hold of an arm. "But I'll come and do what I can," he stammered hastily.

As the little group entered the stables area,

Maisie spotted Sparrow and hurried to meet them.

"Sparrow!" she cried. "What are you doing here? Are these your friends? The Baker Street Boys?"

"*He*'s not," said Sparrow, pointing at Sam.

"Oh yes," she said, "I remember Slippery Sam." Her lips twitched as she tried to keep a straight face. "How's your bum?" she asked him.

Sam's face went bright red. He mumbled something about it being all right now.

"So this must be Dr Watson," she went on. "I'm Maisie, Sparrow's friend."

"And Major Lee's daughter, I believe," the doctor replied. "I take it your father has not informed the police about Silver Star?"

"He couldn't, could he?" said Sparrow. "Not without givin' the game away."

"He's been in a foul mood since he discovered Star was missing," said Maisie, "but there's nothing he can do. Where is Star? Is he all right?"

"He's fine," said Sparrow. "Here he comes now, with Wiggins and Gertie."

"Here? What's he doing here?"

Maisie turned and saw Star approaching, led

by Wiggins and with Gertie in the saddle. Her mouth fell open in surprise.

"It's the only way we can get the inspector to see him in time," explained Queenie.

Behind them, trainers and stable lads were getting their horses ready for the big race. Fred was helping the champion jockey, Willie Carforth, into the saddle on the disguised Blackie. The painted star and socks shone white in the sunlight, looking very realistic. Fred stepped back as Major Lee and Hogg led the horse away, heading for the parade ring.

As Blackie and the trainers left the area, Fred looked round and saw Star and the Boys. He let out a cry and came rushing across to them.

"What's this?" he yelled. "You've found him! You've brought him back! Good lad, Birdie!" He grabbed at Maisie. "Quick, get the silks for me. I can still ride him in the race. I can win the Prince's Cup! Go on!"

Maisie looked at Wiggins, unsure what to do. He nodded and waved her on, and she ran to collect the brightly coloured silk shirt and hat from her suitcase. Fred threw off his jacket and started to strip off his shirt.

All the time, Sam was staring at him intently. Then he let out a sudden shout. "Gotcha! It's him! He's the one!"

"What you talking about?" Wiggins demanded.

"It was him I saw in the woods that night!" cried Sam.

"The night Tommie was killed?" asked Gertie.

"Yes. I swear it. It was him!"

Fred swung round at Sam, his eyes blazing with fury.

"You shut your mouth," he snarled. "Or I'll shut it for you. Nobody's gonna believe a lyin' weasel like you anyway."

"That's quite enough," the doctor said calmly. "We don't need abuse like that."

Fred screamed with rage and hurled himself at Sam. He moved quickly, but Beaver was quicker. Before Fred could reach Sam, Beaver grabbed the stable lad from behind, wrapped both arms around him and held him so tight he could barely breathe. When Fred tried to kick, Shiner grabbed his legs.

"Now what do we do?" asked Rosie.

"We lock him up," said Wiggins. "Till after the race. Beaver, Shiner, put him in that empty loose box over there. See if you can find a bit of rope or some leather reins to tie him up with."

"Get off me! Lemme go!" Fred squawked. "You're gonna regret this. You—"

"'Scuse me, Doctor," said Queenie. She quickly tweaked the handkerchief out of his breast pocket and stuffed it into Fred's mouth to shut him up. Beaver, always as strong as an ox, lifted Fred off his feet, and he and Shiner carried him across to the loose box. Just as they got him inside, Maisie came running back with the silks.

"What's going on?" she asked.

"He murdered Tommie," Wiggins told her.

"Murdered…? Fred…?" Maisie gasped.

"That's right. We're locking him up till we can hand him over to the coppers."

"But … but if he's locked up, who's going to ride Star?"

There was a pause, then Gertie spoke up.

"I am," she announced. "Give me that shirt and cap. Quick!"

* * *

159

Sparrow looked every inch a stable lad in his breeches and flat cap as he led Star and Gertie into the parade ring. The other horses were already on their way out and Gertie was only just in time to join the line heading towards the start. The major and Hogg spotted them as they left the ring and their eyes widened in shock, but with thousands of race-goers looking on, it was too late to do anything about it. They could only watch helplessly, wondering what on earth was going on.

The official starter raised his flag and called the jockeys into line behind the tape stretched across the track. Gertie could feel Star trembling with excitement, raring to go as they took their place among the other horses. They found themselves alongside Willie Carforth on the fake Star. The champion jockey glanced at the horse, then stared at Gertie, looking surprised.

"Who the devil are you?" he demanded. "Where's Fred?"

"Er, he had a little accident," Gertie replied, trying to make her voice sound deeper. "I had to take his place."

"Huh!" Carforth snorted. "Well, I'll tell you the

same as I told him. This is *my* race and I don't want no novice messing it up. So keep that cart-horse out of my way. Understand?"

On the other side of the racecourse, the rest of the Boys, with Dr Watson, Maisie and Sam, crushed against the rail and looked across at the runners and riders in the line-up. Sam raised his binoculars and peered through them to get a closer view.

"Oh no." He groaned.

"What's up?" said Wiggins.

"Gertie's talking to Willie Carforth. He's bound to guess and it'll all be over."

"Now then," Queenie admonished him. "Our Gertie's not a fool. She won't do nothin' daft."

"Don't matter now," Sparrow cried. "They're off!"

The flag dropped, the tape shot up and the crowd roared. Star leapt forwards with a mighty bound. The race was on.

Down the back straight, Gertie found herself in the middle of the herd of horses, all bump-ing and jostling for position. The thunder of their hooves was so loud that it drowned out the sound of the cheering crowd. At first, all Gertie could do was hang on for dear life and pray she did not get thrown – if she fell off now she would be trampled under those pounding hooves. But she soon got used to it and started to feel in control, urging Star forwards. They were boxed in by other horses in front and alongside them, and Gertie knew that if she could not break free she would stand no chance of winning. She kicked her heels into the horse's sides, tweaked the reins and shouted in his ear, and Star responded immediately. He began overtaking the horses ahead of him, threading through them and leaving them behind, one by one.

At the trackside, the other Boys and their friends were going wild with excitement, yelling until they were hoarse. But their excitement was nothing compared with Gertie's. For her, this was the most thrilling moment of her entire life. They rounded the final bend and the home straight lay ahead of them. All the jockeys urged their mounts on, shouting encouragement in their ears. Some began using their whips to drive them harder. But Star needed no whip, just a light tap from Gertie's heels. Only one horse was blocking their way to the front – Blackie – and Gertie steered Star between him and the rail. As they drew alongside, Willie Carforth glared at Gertie and raised his whip.

"I warned you…" he snarled, slashing angrily at her. "Get away!"

For one terrible moment it seemed as if he would knock her from the saddle. But then Gertie grabbed his whip, snatched it from his hand and threw it to the ground. At that moment Star saw the winning post ahead and effortlessly lengthened his stride. Suddenly he was clear of the rest and galloping smoothly for the line. No one could possibly catch him.

As Star passed the post the Boys cheered and leapt up and down, hugging each other in triumph. Even Dr Watson, usually so calm and staid, threw his hat in the air and shouted with the rest of them, while Sam was positively mad with delight. The strange tipster, who was standing near by, watched them with a secret smile. But the biggest, happiest grin, stretching from one ear to the other, was on Gertie's face as she leant forwards, threw her arms around Star's neck and hugged him.

The applause from the rest of the crowd was subdued: very few people had backed "Black Velvet" to win. The real Blackie finished third. Instead of cheers, he was greeted with groans by all the people who thought he was Star. It was enough to earn him a place in the winners' enclosure, alongside the real Star, but his jockey, Willie Carforth, could only manage a scowl as he glared at Gertie, trying to work out how she and her "carthorse" had beaten him and "Star" so decisively.

As they took their places in the winners' enclosure, the prince arrived to present the cup to Major Lee, who still looked bewildered by all that had happened. Before the presentation, however, the prince had a few words to say to the winning jockey.

"Well ridden, my boy," he said to Gertie, waving his fat cigar in the air. "Congratulations on beating the favourite. I'm sure we'll be seeing more of you in the future. I shall speak to my trainer about finding you a position. What's your name, boy?"

"Gertie, Your Majesty."

The prince coughed. "Gertie, you say? That's an odd name for a lad."

"Oh, but I'm not a lad, Your Worship. I'm a lass."

The prince's eyes popped and he swallowed hard. "Well, bless my soul!" he exclaimed. "Whatever next? I'm not sure that's allowed."

"I … er … I knew nothing about this, Your Royal Highness," the major stammered. "I understand the lad who was to ride Black Velvet met with an accident just before the race. Of course, I didn't know…"

"But you did know that horse ain't Blackie, didn't you?" said Wiggins, emerging from the crowd and pointing. "*That's* the real Blackie, there."

The major turned a bright crimson. "I don't know what you're talking about," he spluttered. Then he saw Lestrade standing behind the prince. "Officer, I demand that you arrest this ragamuffin for slander."

"One moment, gentlemen, if you please," a new voice cut in. It was a familiar voice, and it carried the ring of authority. The Indian tipster had pushed his way to the front. He delved into his flowing robe and brought out a bottle and a rag. "Wiggins, my friend, you may find this useful."

"Mr Holmes! What are you doing here?"

"Keeping an eye on you," said the Indian, in what was undoubtedly Sherlock Holmes's voice. "Here, take this and use it."

"What is it?"

"Turpentine, my boy. It dissolves paint."

"Ah, I get you," said Wiggins with a grin. "Right."

He pulled the cork from the bottle, poured some of its contents onto the rag and gently smoothed it on the front of Star's nose, while Gertie stroked the horse's neck and made soothing noises. Gradually the black paint began to wipe off, and the famous white star showed through, to gasps of astonishment all round.

"Well I never!" cried the prince. "Extraordinary! This is better than the conjuror we had at Windsor last Christmas. Inspector, do your duty. I think we all know who you need to arrest."

"Beg y'pardon, Inspector," said Wiggins, "but

the major weren't on his own. Mr Hogg there was in it with him. And Professor Moriarty was pulling their strings. Oh, and by the way, Inspector, we caught the murderer for you. We got him locked up in the stables. He killed Tommie the stable lad, so you can let Gertie's dad go. He's innocent. You said we had to prove it, so we have."

Later that day, as had become the tradition on such occasions, Mr Holmes treated the Boys to a feast to celebrate their success in solving the case. They chose to hold it in the restaurant at Alexandra Palace, looking out over the empty racecourse. The prince had left, and so had Inspector Lestrade, but Mr Gorman and his wife were invited as special guests. So too was Maisie, though she was still shocked and upset at her father's arrest. Slippery Sam had slipped away when he thought that the inspector might come back, so the Boys had not been able to find him to invite him, too.

Mr Holmes had changed out of his Indian disguise, though there were still traces of the dark stain he had used on his face and hands.

"Dr Watson said you was in Germany," Wiggins told him.

"So I was. But I came back, and as I said, I have been keeping an eye on you. You have done very well. Sparrow, are you still sore after those riding lessons?"

"How did you know…?" Sparrow was puzzled. And then his face cleared. "The old knife sharpener!" he cried. "That was you!"

"A simple ruse." Mr Holmes laughed. "But it enabled me to see what was going on in those stables. And after what you have told me now, I understand why Tommie was killed. Wiggins, perhaps you would care to explain the last piece of the puzzle."

Wiggins stood up at the table. "Well," he said, "the way I see it is this. Fred was going to ride Blackie in the big race anyway. He knew he had no chance of winning, but when they switched the two horses, he'd really be riding Silver Star and he'd be a cert to win the Prince's Cup. He'd be a famous jockey right from the start. And that's what he wanted more than anything else in the world. Only Tommie found out about the switch.

He was going to tell Gertie's dad and that would have spoilt everything. So Fred had to stop him talking – and the only way he could be sure of that was to bump him off."

"Precisely. I couldn't have put it better myself," said Mr Holmes.

"That's just brilliant. Brilliant!" a voice cried from the doorway of the restaurant.

"Da!" shrieked Gertie, dashing across the room and throwing herself into her father's arms. "You're free!"

"I am, so I am." Patrick grinned. "And it's all thanks to you and your friends. God bless you all! God bless the Baker Street Boys!"

Back in HQ that night, the Boys were all in their beds, sound asleep after eating their fill in the fancy restaurant. All, that is, apart from Beaver, who sat at the big table staring at a blank exercise book and sucking a pencil. Queenie was awake too. She crept across to look at the empty page facing Beaver.

"Don't know what to call it?" she whispered.

Beaver shook his head dolefully. "I thought

'The Big Race at Alexandra Palace', but it's not very catchy, is it?"

"No... I know – what do they call it again when you swap horses?"

"A ringer?"

"Yes. What about 'The Case of the Racehorse Ringer'?" she suggested.

Beaver gave a big smile. "Thanks. That'll do nicely."

He licked the point of his pencil and started to write.

ALEXANDRA PALACE

ALEXANDRA PALACE, nicknamed Ally Pally, was originally built as "the people's palace". But when it was opened in 1873 it was named after Princess Alexandra of Denmark, who had just married the Prince of Wales, the future King Edward VII. Its racecourse was in use from 1868 until 1970 and was hugely popular with Londoners.

For many years Ally Pally was the home of BBC Television – in fact, its studios broadcast the world's first public television service in 1936. It still stands in its own large park near Muswell Hill in north London. It is used for concerts and festivals and exhibitions, and now has an ice-skating rink among its many attractions.

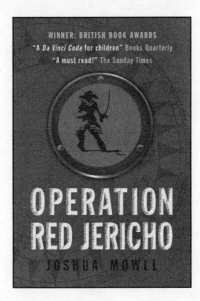

**OPERATION
RED JERICHO**

JOSHUA MOWLL

Shanghai 1920: while on board the *Expedient*, Doug and Becca MacKenzie anxiously await news of their missing parents ... and stumble across a far greater mystery.

England 2002: Joshua Mowll inherits a remarkable archive of documents and painstakingly pieces together the extraordinary events that took place over eighty years earlier.

This is the story of a mysterious Guild striving to protect an ancient secret; the story of two young people caught up in an astonishing adventure ... with far-reaching consequences for the whole world.

**Operation Red Jericho.
No ordinary tale: no ordinary book.**

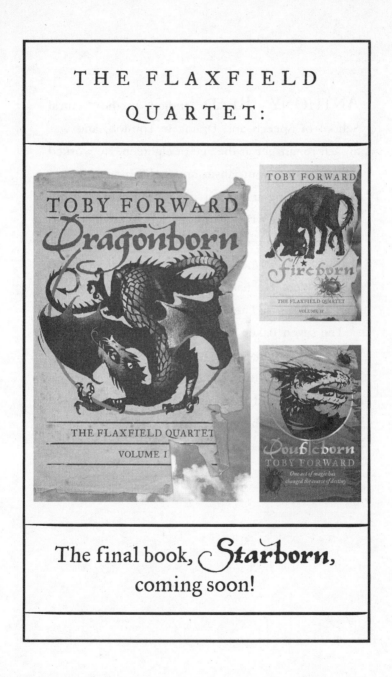

ANTHONY READ studied at the Central School of Speech and Drama in London, and was an actor-manager at the age of eighteen. He worked in advertising, journalism and publishing and as a BAFTA-winning television producer before becoming a full-time writer. Anthony has more than two hundred screen credits to his name, for programmes that include *Sherlock Holmes*, *The Professionals* and *Doctor Who*. He has also written non-fiction, and won the Wingate Literary Prize for *Kristallnacht*.

The seven Baker Street Boys books are based on Anthony's original television series for children, broadcast by the BBC in the 1980s, for which he won the Writers' Guild TV Award. The series was inspired by references to the "Baker Street Irregulars", a group of young crime-solvers who helped the detective Sherlock Holmes in the classic stories by Sir Arthur Conan Doyle.